LOVE WILL FIND A WAY

AMELIA RUCKER

CONTENTS

First giving honor to God, who is the head of my life, I want to thank Him for blessing me with the gift to write such inspirational stories. I would like to thank my parents, LaToya and Major Cummings, for raising such a wonderful godly woman. I would like to thank my siblings, Javan and Amber Rucker. Thank you for always entertaining me and being such wonderful characters.

To the following loved ones, who have been an inspiration to me since day 1, JohnTavius, Bri, Tyshon, RJ, Terrell, Stephanie, Kydra, Rubiera, Ty, Sabria, and Ali, thank you for also being good friends as well.

To my ROTC instructors and teachers, thank you for teaching me and inspiring me with words of encouragement. To my Army instructors and battle buddies, thank you for training and transitioning me into the soldier I have become today. Also, I want to give heavenly shout outs to two women of God, Auntie Ann and Mama J. You two will surely be missed and not forgotten.

CHAPTER 1

"*K*yran, come on! We ain't got all day!" Kiara yelled to her three-year-old son.

"Mama, I'm coming! Can you be patient for once?" Kyran replied to his mother.

Lord, what am I going to do with my little boy? Kiara thought, shaking her head. She was far from a single mother, although she and Keith agreed to co-parent. Keith and Kiara were at one point childhood sweethearts. From Pre-K 'til they graduated high school, Keith and Kiara were the idea of a perfect couple from a book. On graduation night, they both lost their virginities, and two weeks later, Kiara discovered she would be a mother.

Both of them were overjoyed that they would be loving parents, but two years later, the couple's relationship went down the drain due to a big argument. Six months after she and Keith called it quits, Kiara met Todd, a repairman. The two haven't even gone on a date yet, but hopefully, tonight will be the start of it. Kyran really didn't care for Todd since Keith was still a part of his life.

"The Love We Had" by Dru Hill played sweetly on Kiara's phone. Knowing it was Keith, Kiara answered with no hesitation.

"Hello," Kiara answered.

"Hey, is Lil' Man ready?" Keith wondered.

"Yes. He is ready," Kiara replied.

"Great."

"What time do you want me to pick him up on Sunday?"

"I'll bring him around at six o'clock. What are you doing for the rest of the week?"

"The crew is coming by, and Todd and I might head out to dinner. Why did you ask?"

"I mean, a king was just wondering."

"Boy, if you don't come and get Kyran," Kiara brushed him off.

Keith chuckled at Kiara's order. He missed hearing her voice. Her presence made him at ease. To him, a house was not a home without having the one you love.

"Okay. I am on my way. Just hang on tight," Keith assured Kiara.

"Alright," Kiara said.

They had both hung up. Kiara sat down and tried her best not to reminisce the sweet memories she and Keith shared. Dating him was one thing but getting demoted back into the friend zone was another. His sexy smile and muscular arms always made her blush. His dark Hershey chocolate skin often made her mouth water. There was not a single blemish present on his face.

Kiara definitely has many fooled. Her golden honey skin made many assume she was black but coming from a black mother and white father was shocking to many.

She enjoyed feeling safe in Keith's arms, for she pictured herself on cloud nine with Keith. That was all in the past now, as Todd was now a part of her life.

"Mommy, will you let me know when my daddy comes? I gotta go to the bathroom," Kyran stated.

"Kyran, your daddy will not leave you. Heck, you're coming back on Sunday anyway," Kiara reminded Kyran.

She loved the fact Keith and Kyran had an excellent father and son relationship. Kyran would talk to Keith every day. Kiara was extremely thankful for Keith since he didn't break his promise after the breakup.

Kiara picked up her phone and clicked on her Facebook app. The timeline wasn't thrilling for her, so Kiara migrated on to Instagram. She didn't feel the energy she sought on there, either. Todd was at work, and hopefully, he would stop by.

The day Kiara met Todd was no fairytale. She and the girls were sitting and eating at Texas Roadhouse. Todd and a few of his coworkers came inside. Amelia, Kiara's childhood best friend, noticed Todd by breaking the three-second rule. As soon Kiara snapped Amelia out of her trance, Todd noticed Kiara, and soon his eyes were staring at hers. The two exchanged numbers and immediately hit it off.

Amelia, who mainly dated Caucasian men, gave Kiara as much advice as possible. Now that Amelia was dating Nuke, Keith's cousin, she still gave Kiara and Sakitta advice on dating interracial years.

Knock! Knock! Knock!

The knock at the door interrupted her thoughts. Kiara hopped up and raced toward the door. *Good. Keith is on time to get Kyran.* She thought, but little did she know she was in for a surprise once she opened the door.

"Hey, KiKi!" the gang greeted.

"Y'all scared me. I thought y'all were Keith for a minute," Kiara stated, trying to put on a brave front.

"Girl, that fool is at the gas station. Is he on his way over here? You must have finally dropped that fake Ken?" Nuke blurted out.

"Boy, gone somewhere! Don't be worried about Todd and me. As a matter of fact, ain't nothing going on but the rent, which he ain't paying. The only thing going on between Keith and me is Kyran. Keith is still my best friend," Kiara defended, although part of her was fighting feelings for Keith.

"More like your first love," Nuke shot back.

"Speaking of first love, choir time!" Tyshon announced.

Everyone soon had gotten into position like a church choir. Sakitta then hopped in front of everyone. She was so eager about starting her senior year along with Malachi. The two were often mistaken as a couple, and everyone thought they would make a unique one.

"Hold up! What song are we singing?" Sakitta asked.

"Fantasia, get in the Back'! Get in the back right now!" Nuke directed.

Everyone else, including Kiara, laughed their hearts out. Normally, it was Tyshon and Nuke who would actually get the group laughing to tears. Although everyone had moved on to bigger and better things, they all managed to stay in touch.

Amelia was on summer vacation, yet most of her time was

spent training and leading soldiers. Bri, Stephanie, JohnTavis, Kydra, and Tyshon had chosen to go to college. Tyshon was a wide receiver for the Clemson football team. Keith and Kiara made post-secondary goals after graduation, but life took an unexpected turn for them. Keith eventually took a few business classes, while Kiara took a few classes for nursing school. Kyran was already three, and Kiara wanted to do what was best for her child.

"Hold up! Were we going to sing 'My First Love' by Avant and Keke Wyatt?" Sakitta chimed in.

"Yes," Nuke answered.

"I might have a voice on me, but my voice ain't that doggone high. Amelia is the one with the high-pitched voice," Sakitta pointed out.

"Girl, I am not trying to sing that song! Don't put me in this," Amelia shot back.

Malachi burst into laughter. Everyone else joined along. *This is what I really need.* Kiara thought. Whenever everyone came together, it was moments that the group was doing its best to cheer each other up. They were all unique in their own way, and that was what made them love each other.

"Look, are we going to be singing or what? My feet are tired!" Stephanie complained.

"Shortie McStuffins, we are going to get done. Hold your horses!" Nuke commanded.

The front door opened, and Keith strolled inside. He froze once he saw everyone gathered together. He strolled toward them, and a chuckle escaped from him.

"Why are y'all gathered like y'all about to sing 'When The Saints Go Marching In'?" Keith wondered.

"Dang, Keith. You still got a key to Kiara's house?" Nuke inquired.

"Yes, but Kyran is the only reason I still got a key to her place. Ain't nothing going on. We still got a friendship," Keith defended.

"Exactly. Kyran, your father is here!" Kiara announced.

She stepped away from everyone and migrated toward Keith. Kyran came from his room with his overnight bag. He migrated toward his father, and Keith patted his son on the head.

"I hope you are going to be at church on Sunday," Kiara started.

"Girl, now you know good and well that I will be in the house of the Lord," Keith assured Kiara.

"I know that's right. We all need the Lord up in here," Nuke blurted out.

"You need Him right now," Sakitta shot back.

"Listen, Fantasia. Nobody asked you."

"Lying Down" by Celine Dion interrupted the moment. Kiara glanced down at her phone and saw that Todd was calling. She stepped aside and answered it.

"Hello, baby. Look, I won't be able to make it tonight. How about another time?" Todd inquired.

"Oh, that's fine, Todd. Todd, this is like the third time you canceled a date on me. I am confused. Is everything alright?" Kiara questioned.

"Yes. Everything is fine. The last thing I want is for you to worry," Todd assured Kiara.

"Todd, I am worried. We're a couple," Kiara reminded him.

"We're not official, Kiara. We're just talking."

Todd's words shot like an arrow piercing through her heart. From the flowers to the late-night calls, Kiara thought Todd was indeed an angel whom God sent her way to give her the love she desired, but she didn't expect for it to be a figment of her imagination.

"Oh. Well, that's fine."

Immediately, she hung up the phone and did her best to fight back the tears. She couldn't run, as her feet stood planted to the ground. *God, why am I such a fool?* She thought as a tear threatened to fall.

"Are you okay?" Keith wondered.

"Girl, what did that fool say to you?" Amelia interrogated.

"I hate to bring this up in a time like this, but don't you think the three times he canceled your dates are red flags?" JohnTavis brought up.

"Don't worry about it, Donnie McClurkin," Nuke stated.

"Apparently, I'm not Todd's girlfriend. We're just talking," Kiara answered.

"That's it! I am about to go grab my frying pan!" Amelia exclaimed, making her way toward the door. Nuke followed her.

"Not the frying pan!" Everyone else exclaimed.

"Look, if y'all don't want to contribute to the bail bond, then hush," Nuke stated.

"Is Kiara going to be okay?" Bri wondered.

"Girl, no! I am not okay! I wasted my time falling in love with this guy! What am I going to do?" Kiara answered.

"Take it one day at a time. It's his loss," Keith advised.

"Okay. Amelia, I need you and Nuke to come back over here. I do have a song in mind," Tyshon instructed. Amelia and

Nuke strolled toward the group and went back to their positions.

"What song are we about to sing?" Stephanie inquired, bucking her big brown eyes.

"See. You already got Megaphone started."

"Nuke, don't start that mess," Stephanie warned.

"We're going to sing '*Take Me Out to the Ball Game*,'" Tyshon answered.

"Why are we going to sing that? We need to be seeing if Kiara is okay," Sakitta pointed out.

"See, Fantasia even knows the truth," Nuke stated.

"As much as I despise baseball, please tell me why are we singing this song?" Malachi wondered.

"Enrique Iglesias wants to know as well," Nuke declared.

"Nuke, who is that?" Malachi inquired, raising an eyebrow.

"Look, can we just not sing? The song is so pointless, anyway," Amelia chimed in.

Although Kyran saw the moment as entertainment, his parents weren't too thrilled at the performance. Tears threatened to fall down Kiara's gorgeous face. Keith moved toward her, but he didn't expect her to turn him away.

The group dispersed as everyone turned their attention to the former couple. Kyran despised seeing his parents like that. Kyran and his parents still took part in family activities such as days in the park or trips to the arcade and aquarium.

"Kiara, I just want to make sure you are okay. We might not be a couple, but at the end of the day, you are my son's mother and best friend," Keith assured Kiara.

"Where is a church organ when you need it?" JohnTavis blurted out.

"Donnie McClurkin, hold your horses. This is a crisis," Nuke exaggerated.

"See. Now, you got everybody in our business. I don't really want to talk about this right now," Kiara stated.

"Kiara, do you know how many times Todd has done this to you, or do I need to remind you?" Keith inquired, trying not to sound harsh.

"You don't, Keith, but this is not the time for you to be worrying about me. I am going to be just fine. Why don't you worry about spending time with our son?" Kiara shot back.

It took everything in Keith not to blow up or release the tears. A pain crept inside of his chest, but Keith managed to put up a front. His feelings for Kiara would eventually make him explode like a rocket. He never understood why Kiara was wasting her time with a lowlife like Todd. He hardly came around, and that should have been a huge red flag.

"Tell your mother bye, Ky," Keith instructed.

"Bye, mama," Kyran stated.

"Bye, Kyran. Have fun with your father," Kiara told Kyran as he and Keith exited.

CHAPTER 2

"Kiara, is everything alright? I mean, I was trying my best not to be nosy, but the way you snapped at Keith had me worried," Amelia inquired.

"Dealing with Todd is my issue. Keith should be worried about Kyran. What do I look like bringing my baby daddy into my relationship issues?"

Kiara allowed everyone else to stay after the devastating moment. She fixed some orange Kool-Aid since alcohol was barely inside of her house. A glass of wine was needed once in a while, but since she had a house full of people, Kool-Aid was going to do the trick.

"Mhm," everyone chorused.

"What?" Kiara expressed with a confusing look.

"Okay. You said baby daddy. Now, let me break this down for you. If he was your baby daddy, you and he would probably be at each other's throats. You will be calling him time and time, and over and over until you hear *do do do. I'm sorry, but the number you have dialed is unavailable,"* Nuke schooled.

Everyone burst into a thunder of giggles. Kiara was even doing her best not to laugh, but in reality, laughter was the best medicine.

"Nuke, gone somewhere. I almost spitted out my drink," Amelia commented, who was trying to regain her composure.

"He needs to be gone somewhere, period," JohnTavis blurted out.

"Donnie McClurkin, nobody asked you," Nuke shot back.

"Why do y'all keep calling J Donnie McClurkin?" Bri wondered.

"Because no matter what, JohnTavis is always singing a gospel song. I can't ever catch a break with him singing gospel," Nuke explained.

"Nuke, I would rather listen to gospel music than listen to this mess on the radio today," Amelia chimed in.

"See, now you're turning Amelia into Pastor Shirley Caesar. What a shame," Nuke exaggerated.

"Boy, shut up!"

"Look, I'm not about to have church today. Matter of fact, save all of that for Sunday," Kiara retorted.

"Let me tell you something. You can have church anytime and any day. I don't know what new doctrine you are listening to but be careful of what you allow to entertain your heart," Amelia ministered.

"See, what I told y'all. She is turning into Shirley Caesar."

"Shut up, boy!"

Kiara didn't expect the support session to turn into a

preachy moment, but at the end of the day, these were her friends. She knew ever since they took different career paths after high school that a good bit of them were living for Christ. The only ones were next to graduate were Sakitta and Malachi.

"Kiara, as much as we all love you, some of us are far from cuckoo for Cocoa Puffs, as Melia would say," Stephanie stated.

"Look at Megaphone quoting from her best friend," Nuke commented.

Amelia gave Nuke an everlasting glare. Since the two became a couple, Nuke often found ways to get under her skin. Whether she was in the bookstore or with her parents, Nuke still aggravated her no matter the situation.

"Look, the last thing I ever want to do is talk about Todd. I mean, it's not like any of you liked him, anyway."

"It's all Melia's fault. She's the one that hooked you up with him in the first place," Tyshon blurted, standing up and pointing his finger at Amelia.

"What do I got to do with this?"

"You hooked her up with a white man because you like white men," Nuke pointed out.

"And I still like white men, and don't think you're irreplaceable either," Amelia shot back.

"Whoo!" Everyone else laughed.

Kiara started to giggle at the moment. Although she was still hurt by the way she went off on Keith, Kiara was doing her best to cover up her feelings for him. She thought they all had died for him once she began dating Todd. Todd wasn't even worth, or half the man Keith was. Since the beginning, Todd hardly did anything for Kiara. The two hadn't even gone on their first date. Every time Kiara tried calling him, she was always sent to voicemail.

A part of her wanted to tell her friends, but Kiara felt this was her problem as well. She really didn't want to hear anyone preach to her, yet she felt it might have been for her own good. Reluctantly, Kiara brushed the thought off. She sat down and continued to "enjoy" the moment with her friends.

"Is everything really okay? You seemed spaced out?" Amelia observed.

"Yes. I am going to be fine. Trust me. I am going to handle all of this is in the morning," Kiara assured Amelia.

"Alright."

In less than two hours, everyone exited the place. Kiara sat on the couch and thought about everything that happened. She normally wouldn't push Keith away, but she felt she had no choice. Being with Todd was no fairytale, yet she really thought he was a gentleman when she first met him. She really didn't fault Amelia because the only thing Amelia was doing was giving her advice on interracial dating.

Kiara glanced at the clock on the wall and noticed that it really wasn't that late. Kiara wondered if Keith was still up. She grabbed her cell phone and dialed his number.

"Hello," a sexy voice answered.

"Hey," Kiara answered.

"What's up?"

"Nothing much. Is Kyran still up?"

"Girl, this boy is out like he gotta be at work in the grave-yard. Why?"

"I just want to apologize for going off on you," Kiara stated.

"Ma, I ain't worried about that. I mean, as your best friend, I know my limits. At the end of the day, I don't want to see you hurt. I still got much love for you," Keith professed.

"Tell me something I don't know, but this is my battle."

"I'll be here regardless of how you feel. Friends don't allow friends to go through life alone. Trust me. We got history," Keith reminded her.

She wasn't ready to express how much she missed him just yet. Yes, the history had been ups and downs like a seesaw, but Kiara was yearning to be in his presence. Whenever Keith held her in his arms, Kiara considered them a safe haven. She wasn't worried about a thing at all. Instead, she was thinking of a sacred place where it was just her and Keith together.

"Is there anything else you want to talk about, ma? I mean, all I want to do is make sure you are okay."

"I'm good. I gotta go."

"A'ight. Dream of me."

"You too."

Kiara had hung up the phone. She flopped back on the bed and let out a ferocious scream. Her heart began to race twice its normal rate. *This is not supposed to happen. I am with Todd. Keith is just my best friend. He is my son's father. Everything should have died once Todd and I became a couple.*

All of those thoughts were placing Kiara at the crossroad. She felt if she stayed with Todd any longer, then the entire relationship would be a lie. Tears even threatened to fall down her. *God, please show me if Todd and I are meant to be. I mean, I know this is the third time he has ditched, but I mean, Lord, it can't be that serious.* Kiara prayed to the Almighty.

She migrated to her bedroom. As soon as she reached it, Kiara made her way toward the bed and formed up in a fetal position. Slowly but surely, her eyes began to close.

The sun shone its beautiful rays on her face. Kiara opened her beautiful chocolate eyes and sluggishly moved. Finally, a new day has come, but the morning in her opinion, was the busiest time of the day. She hopped up and headed straight for the den. Grabbing her phone, Kiara immediately dialed Todd's cell. *He better pick up, too.* She thought as her blood began to boil.

"Kiara, why are you calling me early this morning?" Todd's tone of voice grew heated.

"What are you getting crunk for?" Kiara asked.

"You calling me this early."

"Let me tell you something. You haven't taken me out on a date. You haven't called me to check up on me. You haven't called me to see what was going on. You don't care about me, do you?"

"Kiara, you're a wonderful girl, but I don't think you are ready for me. One. You're young. Two. I am a very busy man. I don't think this… I mean, give me a few days to think about this. I will talk to you later," Todd ended the conversation.

Was he trying to break up with me? She thought, dialing Amelia's number.

"Hello," a sheepish voice answered.

"Girl, I am so sorry for waking you up, but I just got off the phone with Todd. Did you know Todd tried to break up with me? Girl, what have I done to go through something like this?" Kiara was choking on tears.

"Girl, obvious there is something wrong with him. You are a queen. You deserve a lot better if you ask me."

"Thanks, Mil. Maybe I was a fool last night. All Keith was trying to do was make sure I was okay, and I turned up on him. I am still trying to figure out what is wrong with me?"

"Kiara, there is nothing wrong with you? Do you need me to come over?" Amelia inquired.

"Sure you can. As a matter of fact, let me call Kitta and see what she is up to. I'll see you when you get here."

Kiara had hung up on Amelia and dialed Sakitta's number. "Dear Old Nicki" by Nicki Minaj played as Kiara waited patiently for Sakitta to answer the phone.

"Girl, do you know what time it is? I was getting my beauty rest!" Sakitta shrieked.

"Dang, Kitta! You all in my ear! What are you doing today, anyway?" Kiara quizzed.

"Girl, Mal and I are busy. Why? What's up?"

"Girl, Todd is trying to break up with me. I'm trying to figure out what is wrong with me?"

"That is a big ol' sign right there, girl. You might as well give Keith another chance. The boy did not date anyone else once y'all called it quits. Heck. Most of us are hoping y'all get back together."

Hearing the last statement from Sakitta made Kiara tremble. Although it was true, Kiara wasn't fully equipped to face the truth. She wanted to talk to Keith longer, but that would only make things difficult.

"Girl, are you there?"

"Kitta! Anyway, I'll let you go."

Kiara immediately hung up the phone and collapsed her hands together. At this rate, everything seemed hopeless. First, it seemed as if Todd wanted nothing to do with her, and now her feelings for Keith were playing tug of war. *God, what am I going to do?* The young distraught woman thought.

After the phone call with Kiara, Sakitta called Malachi to get the plan going. Although the two had a unique friendship with one another, everyone was hoping the two would become more. "Despacito" by Luis Fonsi played. Sakitta squinted her eyes, as she really didn't have a care in the world for the song.

"Hello," a groggy voice answered.

"Mal, why on earth do you have that ridiculous song as your ringtone especially whenever I call? You know good and well I don't love that song. You should have played 'Only' by Nicki Minaj. I'll tell you sometimes," Sakitta ranted.

"Woman, you woke me up out of a good sleep. I'm tired of hearing Nicki Minaj," Malachi complained.

"First of all, do not woman me. Second, you might as well get used to it. Third, get your tail up. We got business to handle. Something about Todd ain't sitting right with me," Sakitta stated.

"Ain't that for the police to handle?"

"Mal, the police don't like people like you or me. We got to do this for KiKi. As a matter of fact, I just got off the phone with that fool. However, when we get done searching for clues about that fool, then we are going to head over to Kiara's place. We ain't going to tell her or anyone else what we are doing. You got it?"

"Kitta, since when are we Scooby-Doo and the crew?"

"Boy, just get your butt up!" Sakitta had hung up the phone and hopped out of bed.

Sakitta migrated toward the bathroom and glanced at her blemished free skin. Although she was the youngest in the group, Sakitta was blessed with a slim waist but was thick in the behind. She was truly a Nicki Minaj fan, but she always would remind people she was all-natural. She had ensured that she didn't miss a spot.

Sakitta hopped inside of the shower and allowed the hot water to massage her dark chocolate skin. She couldn't believe she was a senior in high school. She and Malachi made so many plans that involved them spending so much time together.

The two had history together. From playground days 'til now, the two were indeed inseparable. When one was in trouble, the other would be a shoulder to lean on. Sakitta had ambitions of becoming a nurse, but Malachi thought trading school would be his best option.

After the thirty-minute shower, Sakitta hopped out and searched through her closet for a nice tee and jeans. She hadn't worn her Baby Phat outfit in a while, and her black flats were going to do the trick. She decided to wear her long, curly natural hair in a high bun. She even applied clear lip gloss on her lips. She grabbed her purse just in case she and Malachi grabbed something to eat.

As soon as Sakitta opened the door, she froze once she saw Malachi.

"You're here early," Sakitta stated.

"Well, we are on a mission to help our friend. I don't want to have you waiting all day. I ain't going to lie, but truth be told, for us to be 'detectives', you sure do look cute," Malachi complimented.

"Thank you," Sakitta answered.

Sakitta did her best to control her blushing smile. Whenever Malachi complimented her, Sakitta felt butterflies forming in her stomach. If another guy complimented her, Sakitta would not even express a smile on her face. Obviously, it was different when your best friend complimented you.

The two migrated toward the car and hopped inside. Before putting the key into the ignition, Malachi glanced over at Sakitta, who was checking her phone.

Dang. Every time I see her, she is getting more and more beautiful every day. Every time I see her, my heart skips a lot of beats. God, she is my best friend, but I don't want to get my hopes up because she would probably want to remain friends. Malachi thought to himself.

He put the key into the ignition, slowly backed out of the driveway, and drove straight to their destination.

"Girl, can you believe this fool wants to break up with me? Why was I ignoring all the signs?" Kiara complained.

"Kiara, please don't be like these foolish girls once the Lord gives them a sign about the man they are with and completely ignores it. Don't beg that fool. Don't call that fool. You will end up being a fool," Tyshon advised.

"Tyshon, tomorrow is Sunday, and hear you go talking about God. I don't want anyone preaching to me at the moment," Kiara protested.

"Kiara, what has gotten into you? You called everybody over here for support, and now you're upset because Tyshon mentioned God. Okay, I get Tyshon can get fanatic now and then, but he is not wrong. You should know I have love for God. You need friends that are going to encourage you and not sugarcoat."

Kiara didn't expect her friends to give her a sermon. She knew they were always talking about God, so the last thing Kiara wanted to do was go off on them.

"Look, Melia. I am at a crossroads. Okay. I am still trying to figure out what is going on with Todd. Better yet, I need to figure out what is wrong with me," Kiara whined.

"Girl, ain't nothing wrong with you. Obviously, there is something wrong with Todd."

"Quit lying to the girl, Amelia. Obviously, something is wrong with Kiara. She is worried about a fool that is not in love with her, and the moment she said crossroads, I thought about Bone Thugz N Harmony. See ya at the crossroads, crossroads! See ya at the crossroads!" Tyshon started to sing.

Everyone but Kiara joined in with Tyshon. Truth be told, Kiara was relieved that the truth was not discovered. She was at the crossroads, facing her feelings for Keith. She felt alone whenever she was at the crossroads, and at the end of the day, it was she.

"Look. I know y'all are trying to make me laugh, but this is something I have to face alone. Y'all probably have something better going on," Kiara assured her friends.

"Oh, no, you're not going through this alone. God is going to get you through this. We will be by your side with prayer and words of encouragement. Maybe a comedy show by Tyshon, but the last thing we need to see is you losing your life through a man. You have a little boy to raise. He needs you," JohnTavis reminded Kiara.

Bang! Bang! Bang!

The noise at the door startled everyone. Kiara migrated to the door and glanced through the peephole. She noticed Sakitta and Malachi standing outside the door.

"Girl, we got something to tell you, and you might want to sit down for this one. I mean, I don't want you feeling like we are fabricating, but Mal and I saw Todd's car parked right outside of Blue Flame," Sakitta informed.

"Fred and Daphne, y'all ain't even old enough to go to Blue Flame," Tyshon blurted out.

"Boy, ain't nobody trying to go inside of Blue Flame. Everybody is trying to hit up Magic City after graduation," Sakitta shot back.

"Not everybody! You know good, and well, I don't do clubs. A queen celebrates different," Amelia chimed in.

"Okay, y'all. Now is not the point to argue. My question is what is he doing at Blue Flame? Ain't nothing there but strippers," Kiara pointed out.

"That is a good point. He got himself a fine girl. Instead, he's chasing after these girls that will do anything strange for some change," Tyshon stated.

"Tyshon, he broke up with me. A pretty face and a nice body do not keep a man. He can have those tricks in the strip clubs. I'm going to be alright."

A lump began to strangle Kiara's throat. She struggled to fight back the tears, but the news was too much to handle.

CHAPTER 3

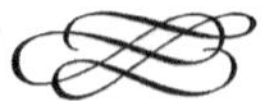

"Kyran, come on, son. Your favorite movie is on," Keith told Kyran.

"Yes, sir," Kyran responded.

Kyran migrated toward the den. Ever since he and Kiara had gone their separate ways, Keith did all of his focus on raising Kyran. Keith called every night to make sure Kyran was well. Even though he missed being around Kiara, Kyran was Keith's main priority.

The Lion King 2 was definitely a fan favorite of the group, since Amelia was the one who got Kyran hooked. Amelia would often tease Kiara and Keith that they were the human versions of Kiara and Kovu. They both denied it, but their friends would insist it was true.

Watching the movie, Keith tried to keep his mind on it, but Kiara kept crossing his mind. It wasn't peaceful that he missed her presence. He missed holding her in those powerful arms of his. She was definitely his peace whenever storms tried to tear him down. No matter what he tried to do, Keith couldn't figure out why he couldn't erase her out of his mind. *God, what am I doing wrong? Why won't Kiara escape my mind?*

"Dad, are you okay? You haven't said a word since earlier. Do you miss mom?" Kyran interrogated.

Keith froze, for he never thought Kyran would see his father juggling with motions. Keith didn't want to fabricate to Kyran, but it was even obvious that a child under the age of five would not only ask but observe his motives.

"Your mother is always on my mind, Kyran. To tell you the truth, I'm actually worried about her. I know I shouldn't do this, but a king can't help but wonder. Has Todd been around you or your mother?" Keith asked his son.

"No, sir. Mom has been distraught over him. I believe this man is just a figment of her imagination. I never seen him a day in my life," Kyran answered.

Mhmmmm. Keith wondered to himself. He had only seen the man once, but now Kyran reported that he barely saw the man. He didn't want to see Kiara hurt, although his feelings for Kiara never went away. Keith felt he had to get to the bottom of this.

"Thanks, Kyran," Keith stated.

As soon as Keith put Kyran to bed, Keith grabbed his cell phone to give Kiara a call. He felt it was still his job to ensure she was okay. *Please pick up.* He thought as Aaliyah's "The One I Gave My Heart To" played sweetly.

"Hello," a cracked voice answered.

"Kiara, I've got two questions to ask you. One. Why do you

have that as your ringtone, knowing it is me calling? Two. Is everything okay with you?" Keith wondered.

"Keith, I really don't want to talk about it right now. Why are you even calling me?"

"Dang. I can't even check on you to see if you are good," Keith stated, yet he didn't want to admit Kiara's harsh words took a jab at his heart. Keith didn't want to start an argument and wake up Kyran.

"Why check on me if we're not a couple?"

"You are my son's mother. Kiara, whether or not we're a couple, I still consider you my best friend. What type of friend would I be if I didn't check up on you?"

"Keith, when are you going to get another woman? I mean obviously, I have moved on, and you seemed to not get the memo."

"Kiara, the last thing I want to do is start an argument with your crazy butt. Todd doesn't care about you. Another thing. There is no other woman I want because I still love you," Keith professed.

Click.

Man, she's tripping. Keith thought as anger was drawing him to his boiling point. At least he was able to get his feelings across, but the way Kiara was acting had him wondered if she was okay or acting even weirder. Instead of worrying, Keith decided it was best to call it a night. Before closing his eyes, Keith glanced up at the ceiling and offered a prayer to the Almighty.

"Dear God,

All I am simply asking and praying is for you protect Kiara. Please remind her that my love for her has not escaped or vanished into thin air. Father, I love that woman with every fiber of my being. If there is any way for you to allow Kiara to come back to me, God, allow everything to be done in thy will. Amen."

I know this fool didn't just tell me he loves me. Kiara thought to herself. She hadn't gone to bed yet with all the unwelcome news she had gotten about Todd was still making her go crazy. Todd was barely around, but Kiara was trying to enforce her mind to not think about Todd, although Todd wasn't making the same amount of effort back.

Grabbing her phone, Kiara dialed Amelia's phone number. She knew Amelia was probably asleep since church was in the morning. "Ghetto Rose" by Keke Wyatt played smoothly as it alerted Amelia.

"Hello," a sheepish voice answered.

"Amelia, I am so sorry for calling you this late, but you won't believe what Keith just told me," Kiara stated as her leg shook violently.

"He's still got love for you," Amelia guessed.

"Girl, how do you know?" Kiara interrogated.

"Kiara, it is obvious. We can all tell that Keith still loves you. This ain't rocket science," Amelia answered.

"Melia, I can't believe this fool said he doesn't want another woman," Kiara revealed.

"Kiara, as much as I am fighting to keep my eyes open, let me keep it real with you. That man has always loved you. From the time we were kids 'til the time y'all called it quits, Keith never stopped loving you. You are the only woman that he has always wanted. Not everybody has to date after a bad break. Maybe, this is a test from God to see where you really are and what you really want. Kiara, everyone can see how disrespectful of a man Todd is to you. You are a queen, and you deserve so much better than a man like Todd."

Hearing the words of encouragement from Amelia made Kiara realized how blessed she was to have friends she could count on. After not wanting to hear the sermon, Kiara wondered if maybe this was what everyone was trying to tell her all along. However, she didn't want to let anyone especially Keith to know about her true feelings for him. Kiara found herself at this crossroad daily. She didn't know where to turn to, yet her feet were planted on the ground.

"Girl, you probably want to cuss me out because I woke you out of your sleep," Kiara stated.

"Kiara, now you know you can lean on me for a word of encouragement. I am not the type of friend who will steer you in the wrong direction. You need to pray and ask God what you need to do next. I mean, break-ups aren't the easiest things we deal with, but we have to remember that there is a reason for everything. If Todd wants to go, let him go. Never hold on to what God is trying to purposefully tear apart," Amelia ministered.

"Girl, you need to be taking over the church with your messages of hope. Reverend Thomas just doesn't know when to stop."

The two could have gone for hours, but church was the destination for the two friends along with their friends. Both of them had hung up yet Kiara felt she was still at the crossroad. Her feelings for Keith just weren't going away that easily, or were they meant to resurface like sweet memories that deserved to be revisited from time to time?

~

"Kiara, come sit with us. You don't need to be sitting by yourself," Stephanie urged her.

"Y'all, this is my battle. The last thing I want is to be a burden on you guys," Kiara assured her friends.

"Girl, give that battle to the Lord. The more you try to fight your battles, you are going to end up overwhelm. That battle is not even yours to begin with," Amelia ministered.

"Amelia, go ahead and take Reverend Thomas's spot. You giving Kiara a word, and church hasn't even started yet," John-Tavis stated.

"JohnTavis, preaching God's word does not happen overnight. People think it is an easy job when, in reality, it takes dedication and hard work. Besides, if God wants me to become a pastor, then He shall reveal it to me. I don't trust man," Amelia declared.

"Girl, tell us something we don't know," Tyshon chimed in.

Before she could actually get up to move, Kiara froze once she saw Keith and Kyran make their way toward her. *God, I wasn't prepared for this.* Kiara thought, violently shaking her leg. Keith took a glance at Kiara and wondered why her leg was shaking.

"Kiara, is everything okay?" Keith asked.

"Keith, I'm going to be fine. I just didn't expect for you to be sitting next to me," Kiara answered, yet her eyes weren't on him.

"Kiara, we're in the house of the Lord. The last time I

checked is I know you. No, you're not okay. Don't fabricate because the Lord sees and hears everything," Keith reminded.

"Look, Keith. Don't try to act all religious. We know how you roll from Sunday to Saturday," Kiara shot back.

"Whoo!" Nuke chorused, turning back to face the two.

"Look, y'all need to handle that after church. Y'all know church folks love to gossip about other people's mess but don't want to sweep around their own porch, which is still covered in dirt. I came to hear the Word and not drama," Amelia declared.

"Can someone give Reverend Thomas the day off? Amelia is giving us a word, and the praise team ain't even leading us to praise and worship," Nuke blurted out.

"For the last time, the Lord will let me know in due time if it is meant for me to get into the pulpit and preach God's word. That is something that should be taken serious and not lightly."

Amelia, although her friends were fully aware, had a love for words. Creating speeches every now and then would make people inspired by the passion delivered from her. She considered herself an encourager, for she spoke life into people's dead dreams. Amelia felt it was her duty to please and serve the Lord, for her backstory would have many people fool. Even people wondered where the young woman got her strength from, but Amelia would always tell them it was God who gave her strength.

The praise team made their way up to the choir stand. The leader, a middle-aged woman with caramel mocha skin complexion, started off with a word of prayer. After the emotional conversation with God, the praise team pumped up the congregation with songs of praise and worship such as "I Will Bless the Lord", "The Battle is Not Yours", and "When We

Get There." Although everyone around her was getting spirit filled with the music, Kiara found nothing to amuse her. She eventually continued to think about her situation with Todd and how she ended up in this mess. Kiara wished she didn't meet Todd the very first day, but her attraction toward him eventually outweighed her first option.

Maybe she should have just stayed single for a while longer than hopping back into the dating scene. That would probably give Keith a chance to make things right with her, but the only thing Kiara would do was be in denial about her feelings.

The tithes and offerings were collected, and Reverend Thomas made his way to the pulpit. At six foot two, a voice that was similar to Barry White, and caramel skin, Reverend Thomas was known for delivering fiery messages. The congregation always grew in anticipation of every Sunday, for the messages hit their souls with the Holy Spirit.

"It's good to be in the house of the Lord one more time. We serve a merciful God who gives us more than a second chance. See, I don't know about you, but every time God allows me to see another day, I know God wants me to get it right or as some would say He ain't through with me yet," Reverend Thomas declared.

"Alright now, Pastor," a member remarked.

"See. This is the exact reason Reverend Thomas is always keeping us longer than usual. She needs to be quiet with that cheap Salvation Army church hat," Tyshon voiced.

The group giggled at Tyshon's comment. It didn't matter where they were, but church was the last place for everyone to get a good laugh. Church was far from a club no matter what it was called. It was similar to a hospital, for there were people who were broken, confused, and lost. Some members considered the church more like a club because some showed off their latest Sunday's best rather than their compassion toward those struggling in sin.

"If you have your Bible with you, please turn to the Book of Psalms 34:17-18. When you have it, say amen. If you ain't got it, say wait on me," Reverend Thomas directed.

"Amen," a few of the congregation responded.

"Wait on me," a few chorused.

"I'm going to give you all ten more seconds. Psalms is the Book after Job. Now, let me start Psalms 34:17-18. The Word of Lord reads The righteous cry out, and the Lord hears and delivers them from all their troubles. The Lord is near to the broken-hearted and saves the crushed in spirit. May the Lord bless the readers and hearers of His word. You may be seated," Reverend Thomas insisted.

The congregation sat down. Kiara kept her head down. She barely said a word to anyone since the service had begun. She clasped her hands together. Keith noticed Kiara, and he didn't care who saw him. He put his finger underneath her chin and gently lifted up her head.

"Chin up, queen. Better days are ahead," Keith assured Kiara.

Kiara didn't say a word, but this time she kept her head up. She kept her head turned toward the altar. Keith never took his eyes off of her, but eventually his attention went toward Reverend Thomas.

"My message isn't simply for those that are saved or think they are righteous. My message is simply for those dealing with a broken heart. Something in my spirit is telling me that there is somebody here that is dealing with a broken heart. I just want to remind you that everything is going to be alright. I may not know what you are going through or the pain you are dealing with, but I came to tell you that God has not left your side. You might have called on your best friend and received not a single answer.

You might have called on your relative, but again, your closest relative couldn't answer your call. I'm here to tell you to call on the One, who will never leave you nor will He forsaken you. Call on the One who is always there. Call on the One who remains the same today, tomorrow, and yesterday. Call on the One who has never taken His hands off of you. Oh, I wish I had a witness up in here," Reverend Thomas declared.

"Amen!" a few of the members shouted.

"The last time I checked weeping may endureth for a night, but joy cometh in the morning. I came to tell you troubles don't last long. Whatever you are dealing with, God is going to get you through it. Whatever you are going through, it won't be permanent. You will overcome, for I do believe that you are more than a conqueror. The devil is a liar, and you will eventually make him mad when you tell him you are the storm."

The members in the congregation stood up to their feet and began to shout praises. The fiery words that Reverend Thomas declared gave them hope. Even Amelia, along with JohnTavis, joined along with the shouting session. Kiara couldn't help but to fight the strangulation that was in her throat. She did her best not to cry, but the more she thought about her situation, the more she allowed it to overpower her. She started to rock back and forth as tears streamed down her face.

A familiar hand gently caressed her back. Keith despised to see Kiara the way she was. He did his best to control his emotions, for his love for her was never erased from his heart. He wanted to hug her, yet that might really bring speculations to the viewers in the church.

"It's going to be okay, queen. God is going to get you through this. God is going to get you through this," Keith reassured Kiara.

"Stand on your feet. I believe some of us need to make our way to the altar. Carrying the burden is only going to make things worse. Whoever you are, come on down and leave your issues here at this altar. Leave it to Jesus, for He will take care of it. See. This is why some of us are tired. We try to fix everything that we come across on a daily basis. We can't fix everything. We can't do it. Jesus can work it out. Jesus can fix it."

"Yes!" a few of the members chorused.

In no time, Kiara hopped up and migrated toward the altar. Keith along with the rest of the crew eventually migrated toward the altar. Each one wanted to support Kiara, yet some were battling issues that the others rarely knew. Although everyone within the small group supported one another, Amelia wanted to keep her relationship with Nuke under the rug. Everything that had been going on behind closed doors wasn't what she thought she would be going through.

As Kiara was at the altar, she couldn't help but to fall down to her knees. Screams of pain escaped from her. She wrapped her arms around her stomach. Keith caressed her back, but tears eventually fell down his handsome face. This was just too much for Keith and others to bear.

Sakitta and Malachi entwined their hands together. Although their friendship was growing stronger and stronger every day, Malachi's feelings for Sakitta were growing more and more. The future was unknown for the both of them, yet Malachi felt he was running out of time. He wanted Sakitta to know how he felt, but when will he have that moment? When will he even find the strength, for rejection may rip his heart into a million pieces? A tear threatened to fall, but Malachi managed to squeeze Sakitta's hand tighter. Sakitta didn't budge one bit, for she allowed her other hand to secure it.

God, I may not know what my best friend is dealing with, but whatever it may be, please get Mal through it, Sakitta silently prayed.

Reverend Thomas migrated toward the group, and once he stopped at Kiara, he laid his hand on her shoulder. Kiara still did not lift her head. Reverend Thomas kneeled down in front of her.

"Young lady, do not stay this way forever. Whatever is tearing you down, leave it here. I don't want you to leave this place without having to take any burden with you. Leave whatever is bothering you here at this altar. Lord, whatever is bothering this young woman, remove it, Lord. Restore her joy. Restore her peace. Restore the love this young woman deserves. Lord, strengthen the people who are in the young lady's life. Lord, touch them all who may be hurting right now. In Jesus' name. Amen."

Reverend Thomas then hopped up and moved toward those who patiently waited for him to come. Keith helped Kiara up and embraced her tightly. The familiar feeling in her arms brought Kiara back to a familiar place. It wasn't the crossroads, but it was the familiar warmth she felt when Keith held her.

CHAPTER 4

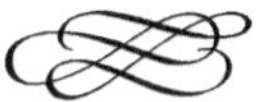

"**M**y question is where are we going to eat at?" Tyshon blurted.

"Boy, I already had plans on cooking at home," Amelia stated.

"Girl, now you know good and well today is the Lord's day. You should have cooked last night," JohnTavis retorted.

The crew was thankful to not have been in church as long as normal. Although she felt a little better about giving her situation to God, Kiara felt uncertain about her and Keith. She had decided to end things with Todd especially how he dropped a bomb on her. She didn't want to allow Keith back into her life just quickly, but Kiara wanted to assure she healed.

"Boy, please. Your grandma is probably throwing it down right now," Tyshon shot back.

Everyone except Kiara laughed at the moment. She was still trying to figure out what to do with Keith or better yet her feelings. Kiara found herself thinking too deep about her issues.

She had no clue how she and Keith were going to start from square one. At the end of the day, Kyran was still their number one priority.

"Kiara, are you good?" Amelia noticed that her best friend was rarely having a moment with the rest.

"Okay. Why don't we all just go our separate ways since Kiara really isn't participating with any of us?" Tyshon suggested.

"Okay. Kiara might need our support, and what do friends do? We support each other," Bri stated.

"I am just doing some thinking. I'm going to be straight," Kiara reassured her friends.

Although part of it was true, Kiara wished she was far away from her friends. At the end of the day, this was her issue, not theirs.

"Look, my stomach is growling. Where we 'bout to eat at?" Kyran protested.

"Y'all, let's eat before Kyran gets a butt whooping," Kiara suggested.

"McDonald's will do since that is our main hangout spot. Let's go," Keith chimed in.

Without saying another word, everyone raced to his or her car and headed straight for McDonald's. Kiara never allowed her thoughts to go away. As soon as she let go of one issue, it seemed as if another one popped right in front of her. Little did everyone know, Kiara wanted to run once Reverend Thomas prayed for restoration. She wasn't ready to experience a restored broken heart just yet. Heck. The one Todd had broken was still shattered in a million pieces. It was definitely going to take some time to love and trust again.

As soon as she pulled into McDonald's parking lot, Kiara found a parking space and parked. She continued to get lost in her thoughts. She felt as if she was on a battlefield as the thoughts were thrown at her like arrows. *You never got over Keith. You were just with Todd just to cover up your feelings with Keith. You are living a lie.*

The thoughts continued to taunt her like a bully. Kiara tried to gather her strength as she tried to push away her thoughts. Sadly, it was just Kiara by herself, but at the same time, Kiara was thankful Kyran didn't witness any of this. She didn't want to frighten her only son. *Lord, what am I going to do? As soon as I think things are done, I find myself back at square one. When will this be over with?*

Knock! Knock! Knock!

A knock on her window interrupted her thoughts. She glanced over and noticed it was Keith. Kiara exhaled and opened the door.

"Are you good? You look zoned out," Keith wondered.

"I'm fine, Keith," Kiara answered, yet there was a hint of heat in her voice.

"Kiara, I just want to make sure you are okay. I need to know because at the end of the day, you're raising my son," Keith reminded her.

"He's my son, Keith. Look. Don't come over here starting your mess, especially after that stunt you pulled," Kiara shot back.

"What stunt did I pulled?"

"You hugging me in front of everyone in church. You know everyone and their grandma at that church love to run their mouths. We ain't a couple anymore, Keith."

The rest of their friends couldn't believe what they were witnessing. One minute, it seemed as if everything was going smoothly between the former couple, but now it seemed as if they were going at it like a married couple.

"Now, what's wrong?" Amelia inquired.

"Girl, I don't know. They better stop before somebody calls the police on them," Stephanie stated.

"Can they just get along for the sake of Kyran?" Tyshon pointed out.

"All we can do is pray for them. That's what real friends do. We just standing here thinking it is entertainment when none of this is humor but real life," JohnTavis reminded everyone.

"Donnie McClurkin is preaching again," Tyshon jawned.

"Tyshon, hush. You always got something to say," Bri told him off.

Sakitta and Malachi, although they were trying their best not to glance at Kiara and Keith's shenanigans, spotted a familiar vehicle. The driver of the 2016 Ford truck was indeed no stranger.

"Y'all, that's Todd driving that truck," Sakitta pointed out.

"Mhmmm. That's that lowlife. Hold up. Who is that heifer in the front seat?" Amelia blurted out.

"Someone get a picture of this. Man, that fool was two-timing our friend," Kydra fumed.

Without saying another word, everyone took out his or her phone and snapped a photo of Todd and the mysterious woman who seemed to work at Blue Flame. Thinking everyone was recording the chaotic moment between him and Kiara, Keith's blood began to boil. *This ain't a time to make me go famous on WorldStar. I want to make sure the woman I still love is okay.*

"Man, if y'all don't get inside, I know something," Keith warned.

"Boy, shut up. Ain't nobody recording you looking like an African version of Samson. Don't make me cut those dreads off. Delilah over there ain't for you as we see," Amelia shot back.

The group burst into a hysterical laugh. The last thing Amelia wanted to do was get into it with her best friend. Everyone, on the low, was probably sick of seeing the former couple bicker. Their only child was probably witnessing this now and then, and that was definitely unhealthy for him. He was only three years old, but his mentality was similar to a twelve-year-old.

"Okay, y'all. The last thing we need is for the police to show up and cause even more commotion," Kydra stated.

"So, are we going to show Kiara these pictures, or what?"

"Let's wait. McDonald's is the last resort turn up, especially since their ice cream machine is always broken down," Tyshon stated.

Keith migrated back toward his car. Kiara hopped out of her car and migrated toward her friends. She wasn't furious, as she had no clue as to why everyone had his or her phone out. A smile wasn't anywhere on her face.

"Are you okay, Kiara? You and Keith don't need to showcase your issues out in public," Amelia stated.

"I ain't even mad y'all for taking out your phones. If that fool had hit me, y'all would have been my witness," Kiara pointed out.

"Girl, Keith will not put his hands on you. Trust me. The man loves you enough already to even think about hitting you," Amelia reminded him.

Kiara stood planted as she replayed the last sentence that escaped from Amelia's mouth. It was definitely no secret that Keith had a lot of love for Kiara, but Kiara wasn't ready to cross that bridge just yet. Her heart wasn't pieced together. It could take days, months, and even years to make it whole again. Little did she know, everyone was concerned about her unusual behavior. Blanking out wasn't what she normally did, but this was beginning to bother those around her.

"Kiara?" Tyshon's animated voice startled her.

"Tyshon, I'm right here. Dang."

"Girl, like the O'Jays would say, your body is here with me, but your mind is on the other side of town," Tyshon observed.

"Look, y'all. Today is one of those days I wished that were serene. Why am I dealing with this on a Sunday?"

"Girl, you can be going through the motions anytime any day. There are seven days in a week, twelve months a year, and all of that equals to three hundred and sixty-five days a year. Rain, snow, sleet, hail, evil will come throughout your days here on earth. We were told we would have good and bad days because, on the real, storms don't last long," JohnTavis reminded Kiara.

"Not being mean, but can y'all not start preaching to me? We just came from church," Kiara stated.

"Kiara, you need friends who are going to tell you the harsh truth instead of comforting you with a lie. You need encouragement. You need prayer. We refuse to see you fall by the wayside because at the end of the day, you have a child to raise. He needs his mother just as well as he needs his father," Amelia stated in a motherly tone.

Keith and Kyran made their way toward everyone. As soon

as everyone turned their attention on the father son duo, everyone made their way inside of McDonald's. Before Kiara could make it up further to the cashier, a familiar hand gently tugged at her. She turned around and saw Keith.

What now? She thought, slowly controlling her anger.

"I'm sorry. I shouldn't have tripped like that in front of everyone. I still care about you because at the end of the day, our son needs you. I need you, too. You are my best friend," Keith confirmed.

"Keith, we will talk about us later. Right now is not the time or place."

Keith gently let go of Kiara's arm. As she made her way to the front, Kiara hoped that the day was soon to be over with. She didn't want to replay any of today's moments or take a stroll in Memory Lane. She wasn't ready to revisit any pleasant moments she and Keith shared. *God, when will all of this be over?*

"Kiara, talk to me. I want to know what is wrong. Let me be a listening ear. Talk to me please," Keith pleaded.

"Keith, why did you humiliate me like that today? You know how people at that church can be. They talk more about each other than they pray for each other," Kiara ranted.

"Kiara, I, along with the rest of our friends was at the altar to support you. That's what friends do. They support one another. They pray for each other. I'm sure everyone in our small circle was mainly there to support you, but some are probably dealing with stuff we don't even know about. Baby, allow me to be there for you," Keith urged.

"Why do you keep calling me baby?

"'Cause I still love you. I never stopped. Whenever I am lying in bed, I ask God what will it take to have you back in my life. I know I was wrong for what I done when we said those things we shouldn't have said. Baby, I want to make it right."

Hearing Keith professing his love for Kiara made her unease. She wasn't ready to even profess her true feelings toward Keith.

"Keith, this is all too soon. As a matter of fact, you don't feel that way about me as you claim to be," Kiara stated.

"Kiara, I didn't came to argue with you. Gosh, that fool has really got you cutting up," Keith observed.

"Keith, how would you feel if I shattered your heart into a million pieces? My heart is shattered because of what Todd has done to me. Here I am thinking I was his girlfriend, but in reality, all of that was a figment of my imagination. No, I don't believe a single word that comes out of your mouth, especially the way you tried to flare up at me."

"Kiara, you are the mother of my son. Yes, we're co-parenting, but at the end of the day, I still respect and love you. I have to make sure you are straight. Not just physically, but mentally.

"The familiar lump in her throat reappeared, yet Kiara was trying her best to fight off the tears that wanted to escape from her chocolate coated eyes. Ever since she had broken up with Keith, Kiara would always assume that they would be at each other's throat. Never would she expect Keith would still possess feelings for her. They had history from the time they were both in diapers, but as we all know, history didn't matter one bit. Although she didn't want to stumble on its path, Kiara found herself strolling into Memory Lane. She never thought she would revisit the day she and Keith entered the battlefield. Instead of the two uniting as allies, the two had become enemies, for their words were the only weapons they had.

"Keith, I know you have been messing around with that nasty trick on Eighth Street. You must have forgotten that you have a family," Kiara scoffed at Keith.

"I want her the same way I want herpes. I can't turn a harlot into a housewife. Who have you been listening to anyone?"

Kyran was only two years old, but the last six months had been a complete nightmare. Kyran despised seeing his father raged as a bull. Kyran observed the tension between his parents, but there wasn't a single moment that the couple would act decent. He wondered when the moment would stop.

"Don't worry about who has been giving me the tea. You're the one acting like you ain't got nobody. You wanna be single, then go on and do you. Kyran and I will be alright," Kiara declared.

Between working a full-time job at the waste plant and being a family man, Keith's energy was draining him like a battery. No matter how he felt, Keith always found time to spend time with Kyran. Keith felt that if a man came up with many excuses not to spend time with his own kids was indeed a coward. Keith's own father did just that, but Keith was determined to not repeat the cycle.

"Keith, Tiffany said you were all up in that harlot's face smiling and cheesing like you wanted her. Go head and be with her," Kiara ranted.

"Kiara, I did not come here to fight you. I have worked twelve hours, and all I want to do is spend time with you and Kyran. Why

are you listening to that girl, anyway? Can't you see Tiffany is jealous of you? What does she have going for herself?"

"I might not hang with Tiffany like I used to, but why would she lie? You don't spend time with me like you used to. You don't cook or take me out to dinner. All you rather do is work and spend time with Kyran. You acting like I don't exist."

"I do care about you, Kiara, but at the same time, Kyran matters, too. Kyran needs all the time and attention that a child needs," Keith reminded her.

"I know he needs that, but what about me for once? I am Kyran's mother, but when it's all said and done, I need to know what we got. It's like you are ignoring me. Is there someone else?"

Keith couldn't believe Kiara was asking him such an outrageous question. Keith had plans for Kiara and Kyran. He wanted to make Kiara his wife and move to a nicer home where they could be at peace than where they were now. No other woman had her name written in Keith's heart except for Kiara. Keith eventually thought about marrying Kiara once she revealed to him that she was pregnant with Kyran, but Keith didn't want to create the perception that he only married Kiara just because she was pregnant. Maybe it was a good thing he waited for a while.

"Kiara, how many times do I have to tell you? There is no other woman I want. You need to get rid of Tiffany. Tiffany is hating because you got a great man, who is an outstanding father to our kid. She ain't got not no man, but the entire town knows she has a different bed appointment every night. I want you! Forget everyone else!"

Keith's thunderous voice startled Kyran. Tears threatened to fall down the young lad's face, but Kyran's body froze once he saw how angry his father was becoming. Normally when Kyran was with his father, his father wouldn't flare up, especially when Kyran got mischievous. Now, it seemed as if Keith had turned into a monster.

"You don't love me like you claim you do. Keith, I can't do this anymore. I want out!"

"Girl, we got history, and now you want to throw it away over some he say/ she say mess? Girl, I had plans for you and Kyran. Why do you got to mess things up?"

"No! Why do you got to mess things up?"

Suddenly, Keith barged at Kiara. The two stared at each other, and even though Keith's blood was boiling, Keith knew not to lay hands on his son's mother. He huffed and puffed, staring at the woman he loved.

"Forget you," he growled, pushing past her.

Slam!

The door made Kiara jumped out of her skin. She grasped the counter, for pain made a surprise visit to her chest. Small breathing began to escape from her. She couldn't believe that it was over. All the sweet moments had now turned into memories. No more cuddling or kissing the man she once loved.

God, what have I done? She thought, forming herself into a fetal position.

The pain was growing constantly, yet Kiara was doing everything in her might to gain composure. Closing her eyes, Kiara sensed a small body near her. Tiny arms consoled her. She knew it was Kyran, yet she never knew he had tears streaming down his face.

"We're going to be alright, mommy. God's got us," Kyran reminded his mother.

∿

"Kiara, please talk to me," Keith begged, snapping Kiara out of her thoughts.

"Keith, I'm going to be fine. I need to ensure that I am healed before I get into another relationship with anyone else. I don't know about us though," Kiara admitted honestly.

Keith migrated toward Kiara and kneeled down in front of her. He placed his right index finger underneath her chin and gently lifted her head. Their chocolate eyes met, but a mysterious spark created a burning sensation between the two. This one was definitely new, since it had been forever for a moment like this appeared.

"I never stopped loving you. Whenever I'm around you, I feel serene. I don't know what it will take for us to be together again, but I am willing to take it one day at a time. I won't pressure you into having sex even though we already cross that point. I will control my temper. I will go to God with you. I am willing to make it right this time," Keith professed.

Kiara wanted to believe Keith, but even though her feelings for him never went away, Kiara still found herself at the crossroads. She wanted to rekindle her relationship, but her heart just wasn't ready to experience love. *When will my heart be whole again? God, I'm just...* The thoughts seized her moment of peace.

Within a flash, Kiara jumped into Keith's arms. Tears streamed down her face. Keith planted a sweet, lingering kiss on Kiara's cheek.

I'm going to do right this time. I promise, baby. Keith thought as a tear streamed down his handsome face.

CHAPTER 5

Kiara made sure her den was clear of any debris, magazine, or anything that was out of place. After the unexpected moment with Keith, Kiara couldn't help but to replay the scene. She missed being in those powerful arms of his, yet those soft lips of his made her aching to taste them again. Thankfully, Kyran was asleep and didn't witness the moment. He was indeed curious and would ask his mother and father a million questions.

After straightening up the den, Kiara flopped down on the couch and turned to Uplift. *Moesha* reruns were on, and Kiara felt the need to get a good laugh. She couldn't count the many tears that she cried for the last couple of days. Kiara tried not to rethink of anything that nearly destroyed her mental health. Normally, Kiara was just fine around her friends and Keith, but ever since the breakup and the recent moment with Todd, Kiara seemed to constantly get attacked.

Kyran was in his room playing with his toys. Kiara always

set a schedule for the both of them. Now it was just the two of them, so Kiara made sure she was fully active in her son's life.

Knock! Knock! Knock!

Who could this be? Kiara thought, reluctantly hopping up and migrating toward the door. She really didn't want any company, yet a little company was what she needed. Glancing through the peephole, Kiara exhaled once she saw who was standing outside her door.

"Hey, Kiara," Amelia greeted, once Kiara opened the door.

"Hey. Come on in," Kiara permitted.

A smile didn't appear on either young woman's face. Amelia migrated toward the couch, and Kiara tagged along right behind her. Once both ladies sat down, Amelia turned her attention toward her best friend. The two had a unique bond that was definitely unbreakable. Whenever one was in trouble, the other would be there to uplift the other.

"So, let me first apologize to you for calling Keith Samson and saying what I said. Trust me when I say none of us were zooming in on your moment with Keith. Apparently, we gathered proof for you, but I wanted to see if you were okay," Amelia stated.

"Girl, he ought to be called Samson. When I say Keith gets on my everlasting nerves, I really mean it. He went from Samson to Keith Sweat with his begging behind," Kiara replied.

"Girl, I hope this boy was not singing "Nobody" or "Let's Make it Last," Amelia stated, trying to control her laughter.

"Worse. This man wants another shot with me," Kiara admitted.

"What? This boy poured his heart and soul out to you, and I missed it? What did you say?"

"I jumped in his arms and broke down. Why won't Keith get someone else when I thought I had someone else? I mean basically all of that was a lie."

Kiara collapsed her hands together. She tried her best not to break down, yet the familiar lump resurfaced in her throat. Amelia noticed her best friend was on the verge of a breakdown, so she placed her hand on Kiara's hands.

"You still love him, don't you?"

"Girl, I don't want to keep getting my heartbroken again."

"I'm actually rooting for the both of you. Kiara, God never makes mistakes. Humans do because we are imperfect. As your best friend and vessel of God, it is essential that you pray and ask God what to do. I mean, God has the last say about everything."

"You're right. Lately, I have been feeling like the entire world around me has been crumbling," Kiara admitted.

"Because of everything that has been happening?"

"Yes. I was so bubbly before meeting Todd, and now Todd has left me distraught. I find myself experiencing attacks, yet I wasn't like this before."

"What type of attacks?"

Amelia used to experience anxiety attacks from now and then. There were moments she would distance herself from everyone. Her chest would throb from time to time. Tears would rush down her face as she tried her best to gain her composure. Sometimes the storm would last minutes or hours. Oftentimes, a new day would come.

"Girl, I am very far from that good looking wrestler you got a thang for, but all these thoughts had been coming at me like arrows. I don't know which way to turn. There are moments I want to black out, but it's not I. I can't keep going through this," Kiara poured out.

"I know it is not pleasant having anxiety attacks. Whenever one is about to come on to you, take a breather. That works for me, and you know I invest in my writing. I mainly focus on Christ and not on my issues because Christ is bigger than all of my problems. He is definitely bigger than yours. Invest your time with the Lord. Do it every day and not just when things go bad. As soon as they get what they prayed for, it's back to square one."

"Girl, why ain't you a preacher?"

"Preaching just doesn't happen overnight. Some preachers get big-headed and forget they are servants of the Lord. Preaching doesn't always bring home a check. I won't be in it for a check, but I am waiting to hear what the Lord has to say."

Amelia did her best to minister to her friends but preaching in the pulpit would not happen overnight. Her brother preached only one time, but it seemed as if he had abandoned it after the gig. Preaching was serious business, yet some "preachers" were teaching prosperity teaching, which mainly captured everyone's attention rather than the true biblical Word. Amelia wanted to lead others to Christ, not to a large bank account.

As the two sat in silent, Amelia noticed a picture of a man with sandy blonde hair, piercing blue eyes, and a genuine smile that warmed up a sad soul.

"You miss your father, don't you?" Amelia inquired.

Kiara noticed the picture of her father, and a smile quickly spread across her face. There wasn't a day that her father didn't cross her mind. The bond between Kiara and Seth was unbreakable. Although Kiara had an older brother and two younger siblings, Kiara always considered herself a daddy's girl. The father/daughter dances were indeed sweet memories. All of that changed when Kiara turned fourteen.

She came home to discover her father unconscious on the kitchen floor. She tried calling out his name, but Seth never responded. A seizure claimed his life. Losing her father was the worst thing Kiara experienced. She would always go to her father, especially when she would want his advice or be in his presence.

"To be real, I thought Todd was an equivalent of my father, but I guess I was wrong," Kiara stated.

"I mean, I thought the same with Nuke, but I guess I was wrong," Amelia admitted.

Kiara turned her attention to her best friend. She knew she was in the middle of a crisis, but Kiara didn't expect for Amelia to experience drama in her own relationship. Although Nuke and Keith were cousins, Kiara knew they mainly considered themselves brothers. Both of them were raised together along with Keith's younger brother.

"Things ain't going great between you and Nuke?"

"No. My heart ain't in it like I thought it would be. He cares about the streets more than he does about me. I mean, I know back then I wanted a rough neck, but now I am regretting it. At the end of the day, I will be alright. Trust me. In some cases, you're just better off as friends with someone. I don't know if I see him as that either," Amelia admitted.

"You didn't sleep with him, did you?"

"Girl, no. My kitty cat stays on lockdown. You have to be worthy enough to be my husband to tear me up."

Kiara couldn't help but to giggle at her friend's statement.

Although she needed to laugh at something, Kiara realized who she could count on from time to time. She despised to see the fact that her best friend was going through heartache, but for some odd reason, Amelia seemed serene about the whole situation.

Knock! Knock! Knock!

More company? Kiara thought, hopping up. Glancing through the peephole, Kiara opened the door and allowed everyone else to come inside.

"Girl, thank God you're home, and Amelia is over here," Tyshon declared.

"Tyshon, you sound like you have something urgent to tell me. What is it?" Kiara noticed the tone in Tyshon's voice.

"So, I just wanted to be clear. We were not taping your moment with Keith. Girl, we were too frightened that the police were going to show up," Stephanie said.

"They do need to think before they pull the trigger," Amelia stated.

"I'm tired of seeing my brothas and sistas being slain, and then we're getting tear gassed, guns pointing at us, or getting arrested when we march peacefully for us to be seen and treated fairly like white folks. I'm getting tired. I'm getting tired. I don't know about y'all, but I am getting tired," JohnTavis proclaimed.

"Let's give it up for Reverend Jesse Jackson, y'all," Tyshon stated, fake clapping his hands.

"Okay! Don't y'all start that mess! What is it y'all have to tell me?" Kiara wondered, yet the shenanigans of her friends made her feel a little better.

"Girl, yesterday while you and Bobby Brown were having it

out, Todd's truck was at a red light, but the sad part is there was a whole other girl in the truck," Bri reported.

"What does this whole other woman look like?" Kiara was itching to know who this mysterious woman was. Technically, Todd was just a wolf in sheep's clothing. Obviously, he was seeing someone else when Kiara thought she was the only one.

"Girl, we can't get a good look, but we all took pictures," Sakitta stated, taking out her iPhone.

Sakitta pulled up the picture she had taken and showed it to Kiara. Kiara took a glance at the photo. Immediately, she recognized Todd, but the mysterious woman made Kiara curious. *Why does this woman look so familiar?* Kiara thought to herself.

"Are you alright, Kiara?" Kydra wondered as Kiara did not look up from the picture.

"I'm good, but Todd really isn't my concern anymore. I'm curious about who the other woman is. It's like I have seen her from somewhere before," Kiara answered.

"Ultimately, that woman should not even be your concern. You dated Todd. Well, sort of," Tyshon reminded Kiara.

Although she was feeling better, Kiara couldn't believe she was played for a fool. Todd was obviously seeing someone that wasn't Kiara. Yet, the woman in the photo had nothing on Kiara. Kiara was blessed with hips and curves that made every man howl like a wolf. Her caramel skin had an angelic glow to it. Her naturally curly hair was abundant like a bouquet of roses.

"I will not cry, but when I see Todd, it's definitely going to be on and popping," Kiara declared.

"Girl, let the Lord deal with him and Baldie Doll. Y'all can look through that picture and see that woman ain't got no hair.

Make me want to sing this song. Have you ever, ever, ever in your baldheaded life have a baldheaded..." Tyshon sang.

"Hey!" Amelia objected.

"Anything else y'all want to tell me?"

"Girl, just know we were not trying to put you and Keith on *WorldStar*. I'm not doing anything for clout. Nope!" Tyshon stated.

"Well, I appreciate y'all showing me this. Keith should be the one apologizing to you all."

Although Sunday was indeed hectic, Kiara was indeed thankful that her friends cared about her well-being. Even though she was still secretive about her feelings for Keith, Kiara brushed away everything aside of her and Keith. Todd was definitely the issue, and whoever the mysterious woman was just brought more heat to the table. Everyone stayed for at least another hour, but as soon as they were gone, Kiara wondered how she could approach Todd about his infidelity.

Knock! Knock! Knock!

The knocking at the door interrupted her thoughts. Kiara reluctantly hopped up to see who was at the door. As soon as she opened the door, Kiara was not amused by the bouquet the stranger was holding.

"Your flowers don't mean a thing to me, Todd. What are you doing here, anyway?" Kiara wondered.

"Well, hello to you, too, beautiful. Kiara, we need to talk. You don't know how much I missed you," Todd proclaimed like an actor auditioning for the main role.

"You're right we do. Get up in here. My neighbors are nosier than my friends," Kiara stated, grabbing Todd.

"You don't want the flowers?"

"No. Who's the other woman, Todd? Yes. I know about her. Who the heck is the other woman?"

Todd glanced over at Kiara, yet his grew wide as the size of saucers. He wondered how Kiara knew about the other woman. However, he knew he had to fabricate in order to string Kiara along. Although he really didn't care about Kiara, Todd wanted to ensure she never hopped into a new relationship again.

"That was one of my coworkers, Kiara. She needed a ride home, and I was generous enough to give her a ride home. Can I not be nice to a coworker, Kiara?" Todd challenged.

"Todd, you just told me in the past forty-eight hours that I am not your girlfriend. Now, you're showing up at my door with these flowers and trying to talk to me. Heck no! I have a son to raise and make sure I am good. You have put me through so much, and after all I have been through with you, I don't want to have any..."

Before Kiara could go on ranting any longer, Todd tossed the flowers aside and grabbed Kiara by her face. He ferociously devoured her lips as she tried to catch her breath. He nipped as hard as he could, giving Kiara excruciating pain. All types of thoughts were going through her mind. One minute, she was in the arms of Keith, and now here she was encountering a wild make out section with Todd. Her heart never erased Keith's name out of her heart. She never really had anything special with Todd.

"Todd, stop! I can't do this! Here you go showing up at my place, and the last thing you're doing is begging for forgiveness. Trust me. I don't want you back, but I can forgive you. You have to go," Kiara demanded.

"Please, baby, don't do this. I know I have made a mistake by not being the man I am supposed to be but let me make it right. Allow me to take you out on Friday. Dinner. I'll pick you up by seven. Give me another chance. I want to make it right to. Please. Allow me to make it right to you."

Kiara didn't know what to believe, yet maybe odd was trying to change for the better. She didn't necessarily welcome Keith back into her life just that fast. She glanced into Todd's oceanic blue eyes.

Without thinking for another second, Kiara leaned toward Todd, and the two shared a sensual kiss, yet this time it was far gentler than the first heated one. Kiara couldn't believe that she was experiencing a moment like this. Maybe if Todd had treated her right the first time, maybe Kiara would enjoy more lip locking action with Todd. After the sensual kiss, Todd planted a gentle kiss on her forehead.

"I'll be here at seven. Please ensure that you are ready by then," Todd informed Kiara.

"I will," Kiara assured Todd.

Todd strolled toward the door and once he opened it, he glanced back at Kiara and gave her a sexy wink. *Dang. What did I just do?* She thought to herself. Her feet remained planted on the ground.

"Did you go by her place?" a woman's sexy voice inquired.

"Yes. I went by her place, babe. At the end of the day, Kiara means nothing to me. You are the number one person, or in this case woman that matters to me," Todd relayed to the woman over the phone.

"Good. I can't wait to see you, baby. I actually made your favorite meal tonight," she purred.

After hanging up the phone, Todd drove all the way back to his place to meet up with the woman. Both of them were on the same page about bringing pain to Kiara. Todd showed no true feelings to Kiara even the moment they met. The day he met her was indeed the moment he knew he caught his next victim. She seemed innocent, but what really shocked him was the fact she had no idea about his true intentions. It was the same everywhere he went. Todd would meet a young woman, tell her all the things she wanted to hear, and leave the girl heartbroken. Todd and the mysterious woman would eventually move across the country to search for the next victim.

Todd would sometimes hit up the strip clubs in order to search for his next victim. Sometimes, he would get lucky, and the woman would appear to assist the predator catching his prey. He had become notorious at his game.

Oh, Kiara. The games are just getting started, my dear. You haven't met the real Todd just yet. Todd thought, speeding all the way home.

"Girl, you did what?" Kiara's friends chorused.

"Look, y'all. I didn't expect for that to happen. I mean, Todd just showed up at my place with flowers and asked me out to dinner," Kiara relayed to her friends.

"Girl, you fell for the getting the drawers tricks. You should have learned the first time Keith had gotten the drawers," Tyshon stated.

"Tyshon, hush. Kyran is still here," Amelia demanded.

After everything that happened between her and Todd, Kiara found herself back at the crossroads. Her feelings for Keith were still screaming loud and proud at her, but the sensual moment with Todd definitely had her on cloud nine. Kiara was getting used to having her friends over almost daily. Instead of criticizing, they encouraged her to make the right choice. Although she couldn't stand the preachy moments, Kiara knew her friends wanted what was best for her. Sometimes Kiara felt God was punishing her because she had Kyran out of wedlock.

The fact she and Keith were no longer together made her fight even more. There wasn't a single moment she thought about Keith, yet now she was torn between him and Todd. What if Todd changed his way? What if Todd was just nervous about getting with Kiara? Kyran was still her main priority, yet if Todd's ways had shown improvement, she was still going to take it one day at a time.

"Girl, I'm going to keep it real. You need to be careful with Todd. Something about this whole dinner thing is not soothing right," Sakitta warned.

"I'm with Sakitta on this. He had better be lucky I wasn't over here. I would have taken those flowers and beaten the mess out of him. I'll keep my frying pan on lock," Amelia chimed in.

"Says the person with the swirl advice. Your service is not one hundred percent customer satisfaction guaranteed," Tyshon stated.

"Boy, get up out of here sounding like you are auditioning

for a commercial, showcasing a product that will be sold in stores soon," Kiara protested.

Kiara allowed her mind to wander. She pictured how her dinner with Todd might go. Hopefully, it was just dinner and not a moment for Todd to get his hand in the cookie jar.

CHAPTER 6

"There you go, bro! Pump it out! Not too hard!" Tyshon coached Keith.

Keith wasn't alone. Tyshon and Malachi were working out with him at the gym. Keith rarely had an off day, but the gym was definitely his playground. It was good to still have friends in a time of difficulty, especially when his heart was still yearning for the woman he loved.

"Keith, are you good? You ain't even said a word lately since being here," Malachi quizzed.

"Well, I'm just trying to get my frustration out. Part of me still loves Kiara, yet part of me wants to let go. I don't know how many times I have to keep begging. If I beg anymore, then I might not be able to walk again," Keith answered.

"Keith, your name is Keith King, not Keith Sweat. I see why she doesn't want you. You begging her like you want to make her panties drop. Heck. You already made her panties drop the moment y'all got a room on the south side of the ghetto," Tyshon reminded him.

Malachi let out a slight chuckle, but immediately regained his composure when Keith and Tyshon glanced over at him.

"Rico Suave, this is black folks' problems, and if you keep hanging around us, you're going to get them, too," Tyshon stated.

"Boy, I'm black and Puerto Rican," Malachi confirmed.

"Mhmm. You couldn't fool me otherwise."

As Tyshon continued to spot Keith, Malachi couldn't help but glance at the couple coming inside the gym. Once he did a double take, he realized that it was Todd and a woman he wasn't familiar with. Right then and there, Malachi grabbed his iPhone and snapped a photo of the two. Once he did that, Malachi sent the photo to Sakitta. Once she had gotten it, the two engaged back and forth on what to do about the situation.

"Who were you taking a picture of?"

"Trouble at nine o'clock," Malachi noted.

"Who's trouble?"

Malachi quickly migrated toward the other two and showed them the picture. Keith immediately recognized Todd, but there was something about the lady that he couldn't place around. She seemed very familiar to him, yet from where?

"Why she ain't got no hair? Where did they come from? Tyshon wondered.

"Forget where they come from. Where they at?" Keith jumped from the bar.

His blood pressure was boiling, yet Keith wanted to throw hands on him. Seeing Todd, especially after everything he had done to Kiara, made Keith wanted to do more than throw blows at Todd.

"Calm down, Keith! You got a son. Kyran needs you. Todd ain't worth sitting in a jail cell," Tyshon stated.

"I don't want that clown around my son! Todd is already on my bad side because of what he has done to Kiara. I can't let her go. I just can't let her go!"

The majority of everyone, who was working out, had their eyes glued to Keith. Keith wanted to work out his issues, not cause a major scene in public. He inhaled and exhaled rapidly.

"He's not worth it, Keith. Trust us. We know it," Malachi remarked.

As soon as Keith spotted Todd and the woman working out, Keith barged over there. Malachi and Tyshon made their way over as well. Once reaching Todd and the woman, Keith stood there ready for his opponent to face him. Todd took a glance at Keith once he saw Keith standing to the side.

"Keith, I never thought I would see you here. What brings you here?" Todd inquired.

"You had better stay far away from Kiara and my son. You ain't nothing but a snake! Who is she? The last time I checked, you're supposed to be talking to my ex, but I see someone's snake can't get enough searching for food. If I see you coming around Kiara, I swear—"

"Keith, I don't think that will be easy. You see I have a very important engagement with Kiara. Dinner at her favorite restaurant and then probably late-night chat. You couldn't even make her happy," Todd boasted in a sly tone.

Smack!

Keith's fist met Todd's eye in a swift. Tyshon and Malachi

immediately moved Keith away before anything else went wrong. The woman, who was assisting Todd, glanced back at Keith. She shook her head, for she felt Todd couldn't stand up for himself. *God, why am I with this man?* She wondered.

As soon as everyone was outside, Keith felt remorseful after punching Todd. Thankfully, he didn't do any more damages to the man, but at least Keith's anger was beginning to calm down. His fist wasn't sore, yet Keith wanted to do more to Todd. After spatting out Kiara's name, that was all it took for Keith to retaliate against Todd.

"Keith, I hate to tell you this, but that wasn't called for. Them folks in the gym could have called the police on you," Tyshon scoffed.

"That fool spat out Kiara's name, and y'all should already know how I feel about this fool on—"

"Don't even use the Lord's name in vain, bro," Tyshon warned.

"You're right. I have to let it go," Keith reluctantly agreed.

"Since we're out here, can I ask y'all something?" Malachi inquired.

"Go ahead, Rico Suave," Tyshon permitted.

Malachi couldn't help but chuckle at Tyshon's humor but knowing that Keith was still heated over the incident, Malachi kept it at a minimum.

"How do you tell someone that you like her?"

"Who?" Tyshon and Keith chorused.

"Y'all should know who. I'm always around her," Malachi hinted.

"Lawd, I know you ain't got a thang for Nicki Minaj.

Mhmm. Rico Suave and Nicki Minaj. I am not about to finish the rest. Well, does she know?" Tyshon wondered.

"Fool, that is why he asked… never mind. When do you plan on telling her?" Keith inquired.

"Hopefully, when the timing is right. I just don't want to rush," Malachi answered.

"Never rush. If it's meant to be, God will allow it to happen. That is what's wrong with folks. Rushing into things will never give you the results you want. Remember, blessings come with patience."

Both Keith and Malachi gave Tyshon confusing expressions. Although he was known to be the fanatic one out of the group, Tyshon was never ashamed about his walk with Christ. Normally, Amelia would be the preachy one along with John-Tavis, but Tyshon didn't mind joining in with the two to encourage their friends.

"Now, y'all know I'm telling the truth. Now, listen here. When she does become your girl, never rush anything with her. Don't take her on the south side of the ghetto and get a room so that she could drop those drawers. Y'all do that on y'all honeymoon. Don't lay a hand on her unless you are praying for her. Think before you say anything that might shatter her heart into a million pieces. You gotta think before you say or do anything. Also, when y'all get into it, take a breather. Never barge or flare up at her," Tyshon advised.

As he listened to what Tyshon was saying, Keith began to reminisced moments of his boyhood. His own father dipped in and out of his life. Apparently, the family business came first, but Keith often took advice from Amelia's father. Yes, it indeed took a village to raise up a child, but eventually, Keith saw his friends basically as family. He wished he had taken the chance to go to Georgia Southern, but that one night with Kiara had cost him a chance to go to Georgia Southern and become the free man he'd always looked forward to becoming. Maybe he would have offered Kiara to come to Statesboro with him, but Kiara, at one point, thought of attending Clark Atlanta University.

Malachi was just two months from starting his senior year, and the last thing Tyshon and Keith ever wanted was to see Malachi get influenced by the wrong crowd. He, along with Sakitta, was the youngster of the pack. They indeed had their entire lives ahead of them.

"Girl, what dress should I model for dinner with Todd? This hot flaming red dress or this little black sexy dress?" Kiara held up two dresses that had been hidden in her closet.

The last time she had gone on a date was almost six months ago. Kiara had the girls there to give her their best opinion about which dress she should wear for her date.

"Kiara, don't take this the wrong way, but have you lost your mind?" Stephanie inquired.

"Look, ladies. I haven't been on a date in a minute. I mean, maybe Todd has changed his ways. Maybe, I should give him another chance."

"Kiara, Todd had another woman in the truck with him. What makes you think that fool has changed his ways?" Bri pointed out.

"Girl, he said that was his coworker."

Groans escaped from all of the ladies except Kiara. They couldn't believe how foolish she was being for a man who didn't invest time for Kiara. Kiara was hoping that Todd was a man of his words instead of being a humbug.

"Kiara, Todd is pulling the wool over your eyes. Why on earth would you want to give a fool like that another chance? Also, you fell for one of the biggest lies a man would tell a woman he ain't giving one hundred percent about. He's playing you," Stephanie went off.

"Okay, ladies. I just needed your advice on which dress I should sport for my date," Kiara protested.

One minute she experienced preachy moments from her friends. Now, it seemed they were breathing down her neck about Todd. Kiara just wanted to have a nice dinner with him, and now it seemed that her friends were going against the whole idea of her going out to dinner. What could Todd possibly do on the date?

"Kiara, you just need to use the head on your shoulder and not the head between your legs. I mean, sex should be the last thing on your mind. You already got one child," Bri reminded her.

"Who said anything about me getting laid? It's just dinner, and the last time I checked, Kyran is enough," Kiara defended.

"Kiara, both of these dresses are screaming late-night pillow talk. Are you sure you want to have dinner with him?"

"Men are dogs, Kiara. They go from one woman to the next. Obviously, there is something about the woman that is making me uncomfortable. Also, Sakitta and Malachi not too long ago saw his vehicle at Blue Flame," Kydra brought up.

Bang! Bang! Bang!

The banging immediately startled all the ladies. Kiara hustled toward the door, for her blood reached its boiling point. Once she peeped her head through the peephole, Kiara opened the door and greeted the trio with a scowl on her face.

"Which one of y'all fools banged on my door?"

"Keith," Malachi and Tyshon answered in unison.

"Man, I ain't taking y'all anywhere else with me," Keith complained.

"Get in here," Kiara commanded.

The three fellas entered Kiara's apartment, and as soon as Keith was near her, Kiara popped Keith upside his head. Keith winced, but his eyes were filled with rage.

"What's wrong with you?"

"Why are you banging on my door like you ain't got no sense?"

"You the one acting like you ain't got none. So, you got a date with that fool?"

"Who told you that?" Kiara's eyes grew wide as saucers. She never mentioned a word to Keith about her date. Her friends were the only ones that knew about her date with Todd.

"It came from the horse's mouth itself."

"Yes, I have a date, and it's only just dinner," Kiara retorted.

"Girl, I ain't trying to get myself involved in what you and Keith got going on, but those two dresses look as if you are going to do more than just eat dinner with Todd. It looks like you're going to get a room on the south side of the ghetto afterward, so you can drop those drawers for him," Tyshon blurted out.

"Tyshon, shut up! Ain't nobody dropping anything for Todd.

Besides, I am going to see if this fool actually changed his ways," Kiara shouted.

Kiara was growing irritated with everyone about Todd. It wasn't like she was going to have a one-night stand with him. Keith should have been the last person to know about her upcoming dinner. She still wasn't sure how the entire dinner might turn out.

"Well, that is what both of those dresses look like on the real. Besides, Todd wasn't alone at the gym either. He had some woman with him," Keith brought up.

"Todd told me that's his coworker. Why are you tripping?"

"Dang. You fell for the oldest trick in the book. Who in their right mind is going to work out with their coworker of the opposite sex?" Tyshon pointed out.

"Look, ain't nothing going on but dinner. You're the last person to be worried about me, anyway."

Kiara tried everything in her might to remain calm. She migrated toward the kitchen and retrieved a bottle of Aquafina. She only thought her friends were going to give her their honest opinion of what dress to wear. She really didn't expect Keith to show up. Keith was the last resort since Kyran was the only priority they share.

She returned with the bottle of water.

"Look, I'm not trying to be mean, but all of y'all got to get up out of here," Kiara demanded.

"Kiara, you're tripping now. Everyone is concerned about your "date". As a matter of fact, who is going to watch Kyran?" Keith inquired.

"I can watch my godson," Amelia volunteered.

"You sure? You and Nuke ain't got something planned?" Keith wondered.

"Boy, I am no longer talking to him," Amelia announced.

"What?!" Everyone chorused.

"Okay, look. My problem is not bigger than the issue that has been brought up to us. Kiara, I will be here early so that you can get ready for your date," Amelia assured Kiara.

Although everyone couldn't believe Amelia decided to end her relationship with Nuke, some questioned what led the relationship to a dead end. Sakitta even admired the fact that Amelia was taking it more serene than how Kiara was acting up.

"Dang. Well, hopefully, everything goes well for you," Keith sincerely stated.

"Trust me. I deserve better."

"Okay, now can everyone bounce up out of my apartment?" Kiara chimed in impatiently.

"Fine, Kiara. We'll leave, but when things don't go the way you wanted on your date, don't you dare hit me up," Keith warned.

Splash!

Kiara stood there facing Keith with absolutely no ounce of regret. She was fed up with him, especially when things weren't going his way. Keith sneered at Kiara, and his fists were clenched.

"Rico Suave, come on, help grab Keith before this fool does something he ain't got no business doing. Hey! Anybody got some Kool-Aid!" Kiara shrieked.

Without another word, the majority of everyone left the apartment. Tyshon and Malachi immediately removed Keith from the hostile environment. Thankfully, Kyran didn't see the intense moment between his parents. He was probably asleep or tuned out by *Paw Patrol*.

"I got a question, y'all. Where's Donnie McClurkin at?"

Although Amelia was trying her best not to laugh at the moment, she couldn't help but chuckle at Tyshon's humor. Once everyone was outside of Kiara's apartment, all eyes were turned on Keith.

"Keith, you need to give Kiara some space. Yes, it's obvious that you still love her, but at the end of the day, you might just have to let her go. If she comes back, then she is meant to be in your life. If not, find someone else," Tyshon advised.

"More like allow the Lord to bring you your Ruth. The more you go out here searching for someone, you'll end up disappointed," Amelia ministered.

"Well, Amelia is right. We all know you love Kiara, but at the end of the day, God has the last say in the end," Stephanie confirmed.

Keith took one last glance at Kiara's apartment door. All he wanted to do was ensure she was okay, especially since Todd asked her out, but Keith had to remind himself that he and Kiara were just co-parenting. His feelings for her were never erased from his heart, yet Keith wondered if Kiara never actually fully let go of her feelings for Keith. He, along with everyone else, strolled away from Kiara's apartment.

"Are you sure you're going to be able to go on your date tomorrow night? I mean, that black eye might be turning her off," the woman purred.

"Look, if you think I am going to sleep with her, then you have another thing coming," Todd replied in a nasty tone.

"I just asked."

"The truth of the matter is we are going to manipulate her instead of making her mine. She was the perfect prey the moment I laid eyes on her. The rest of the time we're here, we will do everything to keep her away from Keith."

Todd was lying back on the couch as he thought about the shenanigans with Keith. Keith was definitely an issue, and he was standing in the way of Kiara. Todd didn't want to see Kiara moved on, yet if he schemed and scammed words of promises, then that would keep Kiara wanting more. He never saw a future with her or any other women he manipulated.

"Todd, I never thought I would ask you this, but do you get tired of losing sometimes?" she asked.

"Losing? Why would you ask me something like that?"

"Sometimes, our plans go left. We nearly almost got caught by the police. I mean, we have been on the trail for a minute now, and to be honest, I'm getting tired of running. The more I run, the more tired I become. If this doesn't go well, then I must say I'm giving up," the woman stated.

Todd raised an eyebrow at the woman. Although he saw her as his partner in crime, Todd never thought he would hear the words that would escape from her mouth. It was no coincidence that no matter how close they almost got away with scot-free murder, the police would be on their end. Obviously, Todd enjoyed making other people miserable, yet now it seemed the woman by his side was growing irritated with it. Until he reached the expiration date of his life, Todd wasn't going to cease. If what he was doing was a full-time job, then Todd's bank account would be overflowing with cash.

Oh. I am on a joyride. Hurting people will always be my favorite pastime. Todd thought, forming a mischievous smile across his face. *I am enjoying the ride.*

CHAPTER 7

Kiara couldn't believe the day had finally come for her to have dinner with Todd. She had decided to place her hair in a bun, and the sexy little black dress was her choice of attire for the evening. Applying her lips as the finishing touch, Kiara took one final look in the mirror and grew satisfied. She was blessed with curves, yet her tiny waist complimented her figure.

Kyran was in the den with a few of his toys. Kyran knew his mother was going out, and he wondered if his father would watch him.

"Mama, is my daddy going to come get me?" Kyran wondered.

"No," Kiara stated without even looking at her son.

After the intense moment with Keith, Kiara did not even want to bring Keith up. She felt he was trying to control her every move, especially since she went on badly about her date with Todd. It wasn't as if she was going to have a one-night stand with Todd. As a matter of fact, this was only to test where his heart really was at. If Todd proved to be a man of his word without having any intentions of lying down with Kiara, then maybe Kiara would give Todd another chance.

Knock. Knock. Knock.

The knock at the door had Kiara's heart skipping beats.

Click-clack. Click-clack.

Her high heels signaled to the person behind the door she was migrating toward it. Kiara glanced through the peephole, but her excitement transformed into disappointment. She opened the door, and a sad smile appeared on her face.

"Girl, you're definitely here early," Kiara told Amelia.

"Girl, I told you I was going to be early. Why don't you look marvelous in that dress?" Amelia complimented.

"Girl, I can't believe tonight is the night. Todd is taking me to my favorite restaurant. I hope he has changed his ways."

Kiara allowed her mind to take her on a journey. She began to picture how the evening with Todd would go. The two would probably skip the restaurant and have dinner under the moonlight. They would probably take an evening stroll in the park or maybe take an evening ride to Southside. Kiara hadn't been on a date for a while, and now the timing was just perfect.

"Kiara, I still don't think this is a good idea. Something about this whole date isn't right with my spirit," Amelia stated.

"Girl, are you psychic?"

"No, I'm not psychic, Kiara. Kyran, can you go to your room for a minute? I need to talk to your mother," Amelia stated.

"Yes, ma'am," Kyran said, hopping up from the couch. He grabbed his toys and strolled to his room.

"Girl, what?" Kiara wondered.

"Have you spoken to Keith?" Amelia inquired.

"Girl, he is the last person I want to hear about. After tonight, Keith shall be history. Todd and I shall begin a new chapter tonight. Girl, don't you know what it feels like to finally be swept off your feet? I mean, the goal is not to get laid but to feel love for once. Keith and I just weren't meant to be," Kiara performed.

"Kiara, yes, Keith should have controlled his temper, but my thing is this. Why did you throw that water on him?"

"Because his statement proved to me that he is no longer worth my time. Keith needs to realize that what we once had is now history. I mean, Kyran will always be our priority."

Amelia hated the way things were going between Kiara and Keith. Typically, everyone saw Kiara and Keith as the ideal couple. Although everyone wished for them to get back together, that was only for the Lord to say. Kiara glanced at the time, and the clock read six-ten. Kiara moved toward the couch, crossed her leg, then played on her phone. Facebook wasn't hitting off a thing, so Kiara decided not to even check her Instagram or Twitter.

"Are you okay?"

"Girl, yes. I'm just waiting on this man to come get me."

Forty minutes passed, and Kiara was still waiting for Todd to come pick her up. *I hope everything is okay with Todd.* Her legs began to tremble. She prayed Todd wasn't going back on his word, yet Kiara had been looking forward to eating dinner. She had fed Kyran his favorite meal much earlier, and she now regretted not fixing herself a meal. Her stomach growled, for it was now getting later and later.

"That's it! I am about to see where this fool is at," Kiara declared.

It was now almost nine o'clock, and Todd was still nowhere in sight. Kiara had no clue what she had gotten herself back at square one with this guy. Grabbing her cell phone, Kiara dialed Todd's number.

"Girl, who are you calling?" Amelia interrogated.

"Todd with his no-good behind," Kiara fumed.

"I thought you deleted his number?"

"Girl, I thought he would find his way back to me."

After mashing all ten digits, Kiara put the phone to her ear. This wasn't how she was supposed to end up on a Friday night. Tonight was supposed to be the night of a real-life fairytale, not a harsh reality. As soon as the other end picked up, Kiara wasn't prepared for the unexpected.

"Hello," a woman's voice answered.

Kiara's eyes grew wide as saucers. She didn't expect another woman to be answering Todd's phone.

"Hello?" The woman was growing impatient.

"May I speak to Todd?" Kiara inquired.

"Who is this? Why do you want to speak to my husband? Who is this?"

Click.

Kiara couldn't believe what she just heard. First, Todd showed up at her doorsteps with flowers. Now, she was on the phone with his wife. *Why would Todd do me like this?* Kiara thought, blacking out.

"Are you alright, Kiara?" Amelia's concern for her best friend never ceased.

Sometimes, the group considered Amelia as the mom of the group. Although she didn't have any kids of her own, Amelia looked out for the welfare of her loved ones. She was considered an old soul.

"Girl, that fool is married. His wife picked up the phone," Kiara disclosed.

The familiar lump strangled her throat.

"He's what? Kiara, I told you that guy was bad news. Todd is a manipulative liar. You need to delete his number ASAP. Let that fool go!"

Without saying another word, Kiara grabbed her car keys and stormed out of the house. Forgetting that she had on heels, Kiara raced downstairs, and once she came across her car, she hopped in and raced all the way to Keith's apartment.

I am such a fool. I am such a fool. She cursed herself, beating on the steering wheel. Tears rushed down like a mad waterfall, and her makeup was now smeared. Tonight was not real. Tonight was not supposed to go this way. Tonight was supposed to be the live moment out of a romance novel. Instead, tonight turned into her worst nightmare. She was supposed to have the time of her life.

As soon as she pulled into the parking lot of Keith's apartment complex, Kiara found a parking spot and immediately parked. Once getting out of her car, Kiara immediately raced up to Keith's building. Keith stayed in Apartment 109, and Kiara managed to make her way to his complex.

Knock! Knock! Knock!

While she waited for Keith to open the door, Kiara did her best to ensure she wasn't looking a mess. Footsteps made their way toward the door, but as soon as the door opened, Kiara's eyes grew wide as saucers. Keith's hardcore abs were displaying, and his black and yellow basketball shorts covered his boxers. Once he saw Kiara, his heart skipped a beat. Maybe this was a sign from God that maybe what they once possessed was never really gone. Kiara did her best not to stare at Keith's muscular chest.

"Hey," Keith greeted in a soothing tone.

"Hey," Kiara replied.

"What's wrong? Where's Kyran?"

"Amelia has Kyran. Todd stood me up."

Keith wanted to rub it in Kiara's face that Todd was going to stand her up. However, something inside him would not allow him to be that much of a jerk toward her. Part of him wanted to grab Kiara and embrace her tightly in his arms. Part of him wanted to kiss her juicy lips, for he missed tasting them. At this point, Keith didn't know what to do, as he was placed back at the crossroads.

Kiara tried her best not to stare at Keith's chest, as going back to the crossroads was her last resort. Although she tried to put up a front, Kiara knew she couldn't erase the good memories she and Keith shared out of her mind. Keith was not just her first love, but the two started as friends. They grew up together and shared each other's deepest dark secrets with one another. He was her shoulder to cry on, especially when she lost her father. She was his safe haven when his father would appear in and out of his life.

"Come on in," Keith permitted.

Kiara wasted no time as she migrated inside the apartment. She went toward the couch and plopped down on it. Not wanting to make Kiara uncomfortable, Keith moved to the other end of the couch and plopped down. Not a word escaped from either one. However, the two stole quick glances of one another. Kiara fidgeted with her fingers, for that was the only option she thought was left for her.

Keith continued to glance at her. Although he was still upset at her for pouring water on him, Keith brushed it aside as he never took his eyes off of her. Men of Vizion's "Break it Off" interrupted the moment. Keith grabbed his phone, and once he realized who it was, Keith answered it.

"Hello."

"That heifer done left me here with y'all son," Amelia reported.

"I know," Keith replied, trying not to chuckle.

"Where is she at?"

"Right here with me."

"Figures. Well, don't drop those drawers now."

Keith really couldn't hold back his laughter, for this was what he really needed. Kiara glanced over at Keith, and a shy smile appeared on her face. *I never thought I would hear him laugh again. It seemed like forever.* Kiara thought, continuing to fidget with her fingers. Keith glanced over at Kiara and kept his eyes glued to her. It was like something taken hold of him that would not stop him from staring at the woman he loved.

"Keith!" Amelia's megaphone voice caused Keith to jump out of his skin.

"Dang, girl. You're worse than my mama," Keith told Amelia.

"Boy, listen. Kyran and I will be here waiting on you both to get back. Now, as I said, don't drop those drawers tonight," Amelia reminded Keith.

"I won't. Bye," Keith stated, hanging up the phone.

He turned his attention back to Kiara, who had not moved for the remainder of the time he was on the phone. Keith, with no hesitation, reached over and grabbed Kiara by her hand. Kiara glanced over in Keith's direction, but as their chocolate eyes gazed at one another, a familiar burning sensation appeared. It brought back to the moment of their first time together, but sex was the last thing on either's mind.

"Are you going to be okay?" Keith wondered.

"I hope so," Kiara answered.

"Can I hold you tonight? You have to believe me when I say sex is not my intention, but you don't know how I miss having you in my arms. I miss the old days to be real with you."

"I mean, I ain't going to trip, but I miss feeling safe and secure in your arms. I used to fall asleep faster that way," Kiara admitted.

"We can lie on the couch. I don't think the bedroom is a good idea but let me go grab a blanket for us right quick," Keith told her.

Keith hopped up and migrated to his bedroom. Kiara allowed her mind to travel afar. She couldn't believe that Todd tricked her. Kiara felt as if she was a harlot, but she had no idea that Todd was actually married at all. At this point, she wondered why she was at Keith's place. Maybe she couldn't erase his name from her heart. Within a minute, Keith appeared with a blanket and a white tee covering his bare chest.

"Why did you put on a shirt?" Kiara wondered.

"Well, I didn't want to make you uncomfortable. I mean, I still care about you, but your heart is not in the right place. You need healing though but not sexual healing," Keith reminded Kiara.

At that moment, Kiara couldn't help but giggle at Keith's comment. Although it was indeed true, Kiara couldn't help but laugh at how Keith said it. Hearing Kiara giggle made Keith feel at ease. It had been forever since Keith actually made Kiara laugh. Kiara took off her heels. Keith signaled for Kiara to come closer to him. With no hesitation, Kiara migrated toward Keith, and once she made it toward him, Keith extended out his hand. Slowly, Kiara accepted his hand.

Keith laid the blanket on the couch and focused his attention on Kiara. Their chocolate eyes instantly were focused on one another, and the familiar burning sensation resurfaced. Keith bit his lip as he stared down at Kiara's full lips. With no hesitation, Keith leaned forward, and within an instant, their lips met in an unexpected kiss. Kiara embraced her arms around Keith's neck while he embraced his arms around her.

I really missed him, but I just want to do it right. I don't want to keep making the same mistake. Kiara thought, continuing to kiss Keith. The lip-locking was lingering between the two, yet they both broke apart for air. Keith planted a sweet kiss on Kiara's forehead. Slowly, he lied back with Kiara.

Thump. Thump. Thump.

Keith's heartbeat was drumming in her ear. She placed her right hand on Keith's chest, but her eyes were alert. Grabbing the blanket, Keith assured Kiara was mainly covered. He caressed the top of her head and observed the broken-hearted woman. This moment indeed took him on a stroll through

Memory Lane. He'd recalled the night after Kiara revealed to him that she was expecting Kyran how distressed she was. She and her mother had exchanged words with one another. Kiara called Keith to come get her to take her far away from the madness.

~

"Girl, you just finished high school. What do you mean you are pregnant?" Bette screamed at her oldest daughter.

"Mama, it was only one time. I just got caught up in the moment. Please don't disown me!" Kiara pleaded.

"What example are you setting for Kenya? What example are you setting for Kenya? Girl, you're stupid! I ain't helping you with this baby. You laid down and spread your legs wide open, so you're going to take care of it," Nette scolded.

"Mama, please don't disown me."

Tears fell down Kiara's face. She thought that her own mother would show some compassion toward her, but Kiara didn't expect her mother to allow harsh words to escape from her.

"Nette, I always knew Kiara would be the main one out of the bunch to get pregnant first," Tyrone chimed in.

"You know what? Wasn't nobody talking to you. All you do is sit in the chair and wait for your unemployment to come in the mail. You don't even do a thing around here. Better yet, I don't see how you even married my mom in the first place," Kiara ranted at her stepfather.

Smack!

Nette had enough of Kiara's smart mouth. To hear that she was pregnant already raised her blood level. Tyrone and Nette met one day while Nette were working at Emory Hospital. He hadn't even gone back into the workforce for almost six years. Nette didn't care what Tyrone had going for himself, but the two quickly eloped and informed their friends a week later. Kiara and her three siblings never even claimed Tyrone as their bonus father. They pretty much just saw him using their mother as a meal ticket.

"Since you wannabe grown so bad, why don't you get up out of here? I don't need a daughter like you that is going to be a bad influence on her two younger siblings."

Kiara raced upstairs to her bedroom and slammed the door. She sat on her bed and grabbed her pillow. The pillow collected her tears. Kiara never thought she would deal with anything like this with her own mother. Grabbing her phone, Kiara dialed Keith's number. Being under the same roof with her mother would not cut it.

Please pick up. Kiara thought to herself.

"Hello," a sexy deep voice answered.

"Please come pick me. I can't be here another second. Please come get me!"

"Where are you at?"

"At home. Please come get me," Kiara pleaded.

"Okay. I'll get you. Hold on tight," Keith assured her.

"Okay."

Her emotions had her all torn, yet Kiara was beginning to feel alone. She wished that her father was around to tell her everything was going to be okay. Her siblings were close to their father, but his untimely death brought disfunction between the four siblings and their mother. Nette never fully recovered from Seth's death. They may have been the definition of childhood sweethearts, but even death couldn't keep them bonded.

In less than thirty minutes, Keith texted Kiara that he was outside *of her mother's home. Grabbing a jacket and her phone, Kiara headed out of the house and jumped inside Keith's car.*

~

"You're what?"

"I'm pregnant, Keith," Kiara repeated.

"Wow. Reality is really biting us in the behind," Keith stated.

Keith's mother didn't mind Kiara staying over for the night. She treated Kiara as if she was her own. Keith and Kiara were sitting on Keith's bed. Fear was creeping around the corner, for the news definitely giving him bubble guts. He couldn't believe he was about to be responsible for a whole human being. Kiara physically embraced herself, for the moment within her mind played repeatedly like a broken record. Keith despised how distraught Kiara was. He scooted toward her and instantly grabbed her by the hand.

Their chocolate eyes stared deeply at one another. Keith wiped away a tear that escaped from Kiara's eye.

"Can I hold you?" Keith requested.

"Yes," Kiara consented.

Keith wasted not a single second as he slowly lied back on his full-sized bed. He lured Kiara toward him, for her head met his chest. He began to caress her curly, thick hair. The rhythm of his heartbeat soothed the storm that was around Kiara.

"I'm not going anywhere, baby. I promise I will take care of our child. I promise to be your shoulder to lean whenever you need it. I'm never going to walk away. I'll be a better father than my own. I got you, baby," Keith professed, kissing Kiara's forehead. "I got you. I got you. I love you."

A light snore escaped from Kiara.

CHAPTER 8

The sun had shone its rays on Keith's dark mocha skin. Slowly opening his eyes, Keith glanced down at Kiara, who was lying peacefully in his arms. He observed her rising and falling on his chest. He continued to play with her hair, for his gentle touch had awakened her.

"How did you sleep, beautiful?" Keith wondered.

"Okay. What about you?" Her voice was as soft as a feather.

"Peaceful. I made sure you fell asleep first before my eyes closed. I miss watching you sleep," Keith admitted.

"I miss lying on your chest. When we were together, that was my safe haven."

Kiara rose, but before she could go any further, Keith cupped both of his hands around her face. Their lips met in a sensual kiss. They allowed their tongues to twirl with one another. Although the lip-lock action only lasted for two minutes, the two broke apart.

"I love you," Keith professed.

"Keith, I..." Kiara began to say.

"I know you're not ready yet, but I want to tell you that I never stopped loving you. I still believe there is hope for us."

Kiara found her way, facing the crossroads once again. Although this time, she was over Todd and not seeking to reconcile with him, everything was coming back to her and Keith. Sometimes history didn't matter, but in this situation, it did. Kiara didn't want to throw away her friendship with Keith or her love for him. Her feelings for Keith were flashing right in front of her. She just didn't want to give in just yet, but maybe taking it day by day was going to give her the clarity she needed.

"Tell me something I don't know. Keith, I might be over Todd, but that doesn't mean I'm ready to hop fresh into a new relationship just yet. Can you be patient with me?"

Keith pecked Kiara on her lips. Kiara tried to hide her blushing smile, but it was no use. She missed feeling this way, knowing that Keith made her feel safe and secure. Keith's love for her was definitely something any woman would envy Kiara of.

"You don't even have to ask me that. If I didn't love you, I would be impatient. I know that you need healing, and I am willing to be standing by you. I'm not leaving your side," Keith professed.

After hearing those words, Kiara felt relief. She never thought Keith would still be the man she always thought he would be. Ever since the two called it quits, Kiara thought Keith would find another woman and treat her the same way, but in reality, Keith wanted Kiara to come back to him.

"Thank you," Kiara stated.

"You're welcome," Keith replied.

"Now, with that being said, I got rules. Do not try to slide your way inside my panties. We already got Kyran. Do not put your hands on me unless you are praying for me. Do not lie to me. Do not cheat on me. You can kiss me on the following areas —my lips, forehead, and neck. We ain't shacking in. As a matter of fact, you're not moving in until we're married. I don't mind you cooking for me just like I have any issues doing the same for you," Kiara relayed.

"Okay. When I tell you sex is the last thing on my mind, baby girl, I really mean it."

Kiara wished she and Keith could go on all day, but Kyran and Amelia were heavily on her mind. She rarely would leave her child with just anyone, for Kyran was always under her and Keith's care. She trusted Amelia, but last night wasn't what she thought it would turn out to be. Kiara moved off of Keith and sat up to put on her heels. She stood up and grabbed her keys and migrated toward the door. Before Kiara could open the door, Keith stood in front of the door.

"What? " Kiara wondered.

"Call me when you get home," Keith commanded gently.

"I will," Kiara stated.

Keith planted three forehead kisses on Kiara before opening the door for her. Kiara smiled before exiting Keith's apartment.

As soon as Keith closed the door, Kiara squealed like a teenager who just received a brand-new car for her sixteenth birthday. Little did she know, Keith leaped high into the air and did a backflip. Although the two were not official, they felt as if it was the start of something new.

~

"Now, Kyran. I have to tell your mother how good of a little boy you have been," Amelia told her godson.

"Yes, ma'am," Kyran replied, showcasing his Colgate smile.

Amelia fed Kyran some Kix cereal and allowed him to watch *Paw Patrol*. She never thought she would stay over at a friend's house, especially since Kiara wasn't present. She prayed Kiara and Keith didn't make the same choice they did on graduation night.

Knock. Knock. Knock.

Amelia hopped up and migrated toward the door. Hopefully, it was probably the gang, for Kiara took the keys with her. Glancing inside the peephole, Amelia was exasperated.

What does he want? She thought, reluctantly opening the door.

"So this is where you were at last night?" Nuke interrogated in a heated whisper.

"Look. You shouldn't be here. We ain't even together anymore," Amelia shot back.

"Why ain't you returned my calls?"

"Nuke, now ain't the time for that! You just need to let me be. As a matter of fact, your nephew is here, and he shouldn't be seeing any of this."

As soon as Amelia tried to close the door, Nuke immediately put his foot in the doorway. Amelia did her best to shut the door, but Nuke's strength was definitely no match for her.

"You better leave before I call the police," Amelia warned.

"They ain't going to do a thing to me," Nuke scoffed off.

Within a flash, Nuke barged Kiara's door open and grabbed Amelia by her forearm. Amelia did everything in her power to get out of his grip, but Nuke's strength overpowered her. Kyran ran to his room, for the scene was just too much for him to witness.

"Let me go! I mean it!" Amelia demanded.

"Never! You must have forgotten who owns you," Nuke sneered.

Kiara was making her way toward her apartment, but as soon as she saw her best friend in harm's way, Kiara immediately took off her high heels and grabbed one while the other was left on the ground.

"You better leave my friend alone!" Kiara charged at Nuke, clocking him with the high-heeled shoe.

Nuke shoved Amelia to the ground and turned his attention toward Kiara. He clenched his teeth and charged toward Kiara. Kiara held the shoe high in the air as she was ready to strike again.

"I see why Keith left you. You ain't about nothing anyway, but don't you worry. You're going to pay for it too," Nuke threatened before slithering his way out of the apartment.

Kiara raced toward her best friend, who was still in so much pain. Kiara despised seeing any of her friends in trouble. Amelia winced as Kiara tried to lift her up.

"Thanks, Ki," Amelia said.

"You're welcome. Where's Kyran?"

"He ran into his room."

Kiara assisted Amelia to the couch. As soon as Amelia sat down, Kiara raced to close and secure her front door. Then, she raced to Kyran's room. Seeing her only son hiding underneath his bed, Kiara reached over and pulled him from under there gently.

"It's okay, baby. He won't come back here again. Okay. I'm going to call daddy and the police. Okay."

Kiara embraced Kyran with all of her might. She hated how things were at the moment for her own best friend. Her little boy was frightened, as his own godmother was getting attacked by the man she once fell in love with. Kiara, at that moment, wished Keith was by her side. He would be there to comfort both her and Kyran and protect them. Picking up Kyran, Kiara raced back to the den and dialed Keith's number.

"Break Me Off" was playing its sweet melody, but the atmosphere was bittersweet.

"Hello," a sexy voice answered on the second ring.

"Hey. We need you. Nuke attacked Amelia as I was coming inside. Kyran was scared for his life. Please come over, please!" Kiara pleaded.

"Okay. I'm on my way. Stay put and lock the door," Keith directed.

"Trust me. I was already on it," Kiara told Keith.

"I'll see you in a bit."

After getting off the phone with Keith, Kiara texted the others about the incident with Nuke. Amelia called the police and waited for them to arrive. Both friends sat on the couch. Kiara realized that she had left her high-heeled shoe outside, but the safety of her best friend and son was her priority. Everything was beginning to look as if hope was reviving in her life. She hated that Amelia was dealing with torment from Nuke.

"How long has this been going on?" Kiara interrogated.

"The past three weeks. I thought Nuke differed from any of the guys I had dated prior to him. I thought I did, but Nuke turned into a horrible monster. I don't want to be with him anymore," Amelia explained.

"Why didn't you tell Keith or me?"

"Kiara, I didn't want to be a burden on anyone."

"No, the last thing we need to do is bury one of our loved ones due to domestic violence. I hope you're planning to press charges. He doesn't deserve to walk through the streets."

Knock. Knock. Knock.

The knocking at the door caught both of the young women's attention. Still holding Kyran, Kiara hopped up and migrated toward the door. Glancing through the peephole, Kiara exhaled. Seeing that it was indeed Keith, she opened the door.

"I hate to ask, but did Cinderella lose a high heel?" Keith interrogated, holding up Kiara's other shoe.

"Boy, get in here," Kiara ordered, giggling at Keith's question.

Keith planted a kiss on Kiara's forehead. Kyran reached out to Keith, and Keith immediately took his child in his arms. He kissed the side of Kyran's head and embraced him with all of his might. Keith noticed Amelia sitting on the couch, and a sad smile appeared on Amelia's face.

"How are you holding up?"

"I'm going to be good."

Bang! Bang! Bang!

The banging at the door made all of them jumped out of their skin. Kiara, thinking it could have been the police, opened the door.

"Where is he? Where is he?" Stephanie inquired, raising a baseball bat in the air.

Everyone else barged inside of Kiara's apartment. The rest of them were matched in camouflage outfits and carried baseball bats. Keith's eyes grew wide as saucers, for he couldn't believe how fanatic his friends were acting.

"I don't know if y'all are trying to audition for "Rhythm Nation" or Stephanie getting too hyped about PeeWee season, but please have some respect for Kiara. This is her apartment," Keith reminded them.

"Trust us. We know, but where the heck is Nuke at?" Tyshon interrogated.

"He ain't here the last time I checked," Kiara shot back.

"Y'all need to really calm down. The police are on their way," Amelia informed them.

"You called the po-po? Girl, you must have forgotten—" Tyshon went on.

"Tyshon, we know the police can't be trusted, but people like Nuke do not deserve to be walking on the streets. Nuke literally put his hands on Amelia, and no woman should have to experience abuse," Kiara went off.

"That's why we got Keith as our bodyguard," Tyshon blurted out.

"Fool, I am not trying to get killed. No, I refuse to condone Nuke's actions, but the last thing I need is for my son to become a fatherless black child. Nuke ain't worth going to jail over," Keith declared.

Although Keith was enraged about the whole situation, he didn't want to lose another moment with Kiara. The previous night made him realized how much he missed being in her presence. He prayed God would allow Kiara to come back to him but missing out on his son's life was definitely not going to happen. Kiara and Kyran were his main two priority.

Knock. Knock. Knock.

Kiara migrated to the door. Sighing, Kiara opened the door, and two officers, who were built like ox, strolled inside of Kiara's apartment. One had the skin complexion similar to caramel mocha, and the other one had the complexion of smooth dark chocolate.

"Good God Almighty! I swear the Lord doesn't make them like He used to," Stephanie declared.

"Stephanie, calm down. This is a serious matter," Keith advised.

"We got a call about a domestic dispute. Is everything okay?" one of the officers interrogated.

"Officer, I called. I would like to file a report on Nuke. This has been going on for three weeks, and today, he came over here and attacked me," Amelia explained.

"Three weeks? Hold up. Why haven't you told us?" Kydra interjected.

"I don't want any of y'all to get in trouble," Amelia explained.

"Get in trouble for what? The last thing we need is to bury you because a punk put his hands on you. He needs to be locked up, and y'all don't need to let him out," Tyshon went off.

"Miss, can you please tell us his name?"

"How about y'all just tell her y'all names?" Stephanie suggested.

"Stephanie, calm your hormones down. These brothas are probably married."

The officers chuckled slightly at the comment, but they swiftly turned their attention back to Amelia.

"His name is Nuke King. He is six foot two. An athletic built body, dark-skinned, dreads, and drives an expensive 2016 Jaguar," Amelia described.

"As in Nuke King the plug?"

"The plug? What do you mean the plug?"

"Well, we actually have a warrant for his arrest. Thankfully, you have provided us with the information. Also, if I were you, I would get a restraining order. As a matter of fact, we will file one for you. Here is our card," the officer stated, handing Amelia a business card.

Amelia took the card and placed it in her pocket. The officers were just turning to leave, but Stephanie raced toward the door. She blocked the entrance, and both officers along with her friends expressed confusion on their faces.

"Miss, we're about to leave. Is everything okay?"

"Officers, just go ahead and place me in handcuffs. Did anyone ever tell y'all so fine? God don't make them like He used to. Whoo!" Stephanie began to imitate a person shouting.

"Stephanie, the only thing screeching louder than you is your cat that is being suffocated by panties," JohnTavis shot back.

Right then and there, the atmosphere was filled with laughter. Kiara really felt this was the moment to cheer her and Amelia up. Laughter was definitely the best medicine. The two police officers exited the apartment and went on their way.

"JohnTavis, you better be glad that we are friends," Stephanie reminded him.

"I ain't trying to be funny, but that will seem like something I would say," Tyshon pointed.

"I ain't definitely being funny, but if y'all don't live here, bounce out of here please," Keith commanded.

"You don't even stay here," Tyshon shot back.

"I know, but neither do y'all," Keith countered.

"Also, y'all convoy Amelia back to her place," Kiara suggested.

"Y'all acting like we are in the Army," Bri retorted.

"Well, y'all are escorting a soldier today. Everybody, y'all ain't got to go home, but y'all got to bounce up out of here," Keith demanded.

"Says the fool that doesn't live here," Tyshon complained.

"Group, attention!" Amelia commanded.

Soon, the group stopped moving. Amelia hopped up from the couch and raced toward the door. Although she wasn't fully recovered, Amelia was a little pump from the laughing matter. Amelia opened the door and stood right beside it.

"Forward, march! Left. Left. Left, Right. Right, Left."

The group began to move in a single file line. The rhythm of their feet was a unique cadence. Before Amelia could exit the building, Tyshon poked his head inside the apartment.

"Remember what I told you, Keith. Don't drop those drawers," he reminded Keith.

"Boy, get up out of here," Keith warned.

Amelia immediately closed the door. Kiara hopped up and raced toward the back. She decided now would be a great time to freshen up for the night. She focused all of her concern on her son and best friends. As soon as Kiara reached the bathroom, she stripped out of the dress and turned on the hot water. Stepping inside of the shower, Kiara allowed the steaming water to massage her golden honey skin. The water was bringing her sweet comfort, yet it was warm like a person's touch. She couldn't stop replaying the sweet moment of her and Keith from the night before. She definitely missed being in his arms, but she could only take it day by day if she was willing to give Keith another chance.

After the thirty-minute shower, Kiara hopped out and moisturized her body with Palmer's Cocoa Butter. She put on an old pajama set that still would fool many because Kiara took care of her clothes. She basically focused all of her time and attention on taking care of Kyran. Migrating back to the den, Kiara noticed Keith wasn't on the couch. As a matter of fact, she didn't even hear front door shut when she was washing off.

Little did she know, Keith was creeping from Kyran's bedroom. He kept his eyes on her as she had no clue as to him being behind her. Keith raised his hands high above his head and waited for Kiara to notice him. Like a lion waiting for his prey to fall, he continued to creep up on Kiara. Turning around, Kiara shrieked.

"Keith, what were you thinking? As a matter of fact, where is Kyran at?" Kiara wondered.

"I put him to bed. Can you come near me, please?" Keith inquired, signaling for Kiara to come his way.

"Sure. What's your motive?" Kiara wondered.

"I didn't get the chance to hold you today. Or better yet, kiss you."

Kiara couldn't deny the ache of wanting to be in Keith's presence. The other night indeed brought back memories, yet she was still willing to take it day by day, rebuilding her relationship with Keith. Not hesitating, she migrated toward him and allowed him to embrace her. His embrace made her knees buckled, for his strong arms were tighter around her frame. His lips planted small pecks on her neck, for small moans escaped from her.

"I missed you," Keith whispered.

"I missed you, too," Kiara responded.

"What do you want to do tonight?"

"Lie in your arms like last night. Take it slow," Kiara answered.

Two sets of chocolate eyes stared at one another, as hungry lips were aching to taste one another. Instead, Keith planted a lingering kiss on Kiara's forehead. Only then would love remain on layaway.

CHAPTER 9

The sun's rays greeted Keith's dark chocolate skin. Slowly opening his eyes, Keith smiled as he noticed the sleeping beauty in his arms. He allowed his index finger to trace upon her soft skin. He kissed her forehead as he continued to outline her gorgeous face.

"Keith," Kiara slurred.

"I'm here, beautiful," Keith confirmed, playing with her curly hair.

Slowly rising, Kiara moved closer to Keith and gave him a sweet kiss. This time Kiara felt content with Keith, but the last two days have been hectic. First, Todd's secret life is revealed, and then Amelia gets attacked by Nuke. Kiara wondered how her best friend was doing after the incident. Swiftly, Kiara hopped up to grab her cell phone and dialed Amelia's cell phone number. Keith glanced over at Kiara and expressed a confused look.

"Are you good?"

"Yes. I want to ensure my best friend is good. Yesterday was definitely unexpected. Not only did my best friend fear for her life, but our son was scared too. I don't want to lose my friend to a lowlife that feels he has to abuse women. You never abused me. Kovi never abused Kenya, so why does that fool think it is okay for him to abuse my best friend? She deserves to be treated right like the queen she is," Kiara preached.

"Hello," a sheepish voice answered.

"Hey, girl. This is KiKi. Are you okay?" Kiara interrogated.

"Girl, I am going to be okay. Those two knights in uniform really came through for a queen. We need to do something about Stephanie. Her tail nearly knocked down one of the officers," Amelia stated.

"Girl, I agree with you. Both of these jokers were fine, but I didn't want to make Keith jealous by saying anything. I couldn't get over the dark-skinned brother," Kiara admitted, not realizing Keith was still in her apartment.

"Girl, I definitely had to keep my composure. It was the caramel brotha for me. He kind of reminds me of Kopa."

"I know. Heck. I should do my weekly texting with my siblings. Kopa barely comes through," Kiara stated.

Kiara, along with her three siblings, basically kept in touch, but they had decided to do their own thing. Kopa, who was the oldest, was getting his affairs in order. Kion was attending Kentucky University on a basketball scholarship. Kenya was in medical school, where she was focused on becoming a nurse. At the end of the day, Kiara felt besides Kyran, her siblings were all she had. All four of them barely had a thing to do with their own mother.

"Girl, let me let you go. I forgot I still got company," Kiara told Amelia.

"Alright. I will be here. Wait a minute. Is Keith over there?"

"Girl, who else is going to be over here?"

"That sexy police officer you were probably drooling over."

"Girl, slob was not coming out of my mouth, so don't go there. Anyway, holla if you need me."

"Alright. I holla," Amelia concluded before hanging up the phone.

Kiara placed her cell phone on the table and turned her attention back to Keith. She froze once she noticed Keith giving her a seductive look. He then strolled toward Kiara, yet her feet remained planted to the ground.

"So, last night, you were drooling over the police officer, knowing good and well you wanted me to stay with you last night?"

"Keith, I might have thought he was attractive, but trust me. Stephanie was the one who really brought me back to reality. Heck. Melia thought the other one was fine, so those two might as well grab them while they can. You have nothing to worry about," Kiara assured Keith by playfully poking Keith in the chest. Before she could take a step forward, Keith turned her back toward him and gave her a hard sensual kiss.

Not knowing what to do, Kiara placed her hands on Keith's forearm, but the unexpected kiss lasted only about thirty seconds.

"You still owe me," Keith teased.

"Boy, remember that we are still taking it day by day. We ain't even official. As a matter of fact, we need to be careful what we do in front of Kyran. Kids can get the wrong idea, and that can really hurt them," Kiara reminded.

Although Kiara was right, Keith was determined to become one with Kiara. He was growing agitated with just calling his son and getting him every other weekend. His goal was to come home to Kiara and Kyran, not just pop up whenever. Hopefully, Kiara wasn't having any intention of giving Todd another chance. Besides, Todd already had a wife of his own.

"How about have dinner with me?"

"When?"

"Friday."

"Okay. Hopefully, the crew is able to watch Kyran. What time do you want to come get me?"

"Six. Dinner only," Keith mentioned.

"It's a start."

Kiara didn't think Keith would ask her out to dinner. Typically, the two would take a ride to Southside, but that was only memories of when the couple was allowed to start dating as teens. From bowling alleys to movie theaters, especially prom and homecoming, the two would definitely have the time of their lives. Now, the two were working on rebuilding their relationship, and the sweet memories would often appear and remind them of the love they both shared.

"Well, what do you want me to do in the meantime?" Keith wondered.

"What I normally like, mister — good morning and good night texts. You can call me. You can give me foot massages. I mainly want things money can't buy. How hard is that?"

"Not hard at all. Trust me. I think about you day and night.

When we broke up, believe it or not, I cried because I thought I lost my best friend forever. I mean, I wish I can turn back the hands of time, but I can't. I do promise to do right this time," Keith professed.

"You have to prove it to me first, smooth talker," Kiara purred.

Keith leaned in toward Kiara, for tasting her lips was all he wanted to do. Kiara eventually missed those lip-locking moments, but right now wasn't a time to rush.

"Mama," Kyran called.

"Whoo!" Kiara brushed past Keith and raced to their son's room.

Once she arrived there, Kiara fixed her composure and migrated toward her son's bed. Kyran's eyes were still heavy, yet the dream he had wasn't a horror one.

"Good morning, sleepy head," Kiara greeted Kyran.

"Good morning. Is my daddy still here?"

"Yes, he is. Wait one minute."

Kiara then migrated out of the room and went right back to Keith.

"He wants to see you."

"Okay."

"Make sure you put on a shirt. I don't need you showing evidence that you stayed over."

Keith chuckled at Kiara's demand, yet he did as he was told. Before heading to see Kyran, Keith signaled for Kiara to follow him. They both made their entrance inside their only child's room.

"Hey, buddy," Keith greeted.

"Is Uncle Nuke coming back over here?"

"Trust me. He is banned from coming over here," Keith assured Kyran.

Kiara's eyes enlarged once she heard the answer Keith gave Kyran. *First of all, you don't even stay or pay a single bill here. Second of all, I was going to ban that fool period. Relative or not.*

"Are you going to move back in with mama?"

"Only God has the last say about everything. Hopefully, one day," Keith answered honestly.

Kiara knew what Keith meant, but the two weren't even official. On the real, she still wondered where this would take her. She wanted to be a wife more than just having the title of being the mother of his son. She was far from an unfit mother, yet she was beginning to get sick of Keith and her sharing Kyran every weekend. She longed for the day Keith would come home to both Kyran and her, but for that to happen, she and Keith needed to tie the knot. They both already had a child out of wedlock, but marriage was a whole other story.

"You good?" Keith inquired Kiara.

"Yes. Just thinking…"

Although it was partly true, Kiara didn't know how to feel about taking the next step of marriage, but she could feel Keith's eyes staring at her and not once moving away.

"Todd, can you sit down? You need to calm down," Tiffany urged.

"Trust me. It has been two days, and she has not called me back. Why did you have to pick up the phone?"

Todd paced back and forth. His blood pressure had reached

its boiling point. It had been two days, and Kiara hadn't even called back. "Our task is not complete. I want to get this girl to her breaking point."

"You need to calm down before you end up in the hospital. Trust me. Kiara is going to get back into reality. I mean, at the end of the day, she probably isn't over you," Tiffany reminded him.

After informing Todd that Kiara called the house, Tiffany then revealed to him that she told Kiara Todd was her husband. Todd didn't want anyone to find out about his relationship with Tiffany. The two definitely hadn't been intimate in what seemed all eternity. They had no interest whatsoever to take their marriage seriously. Preying on the naive and young had been their main plot. A divorce never came into their discussion, but the benefits of coming home, scheming and plotting, and eating dinner seemed to make them both content.

"You don't think she went back to that guy."

"Why would she go back to him? I mean, obviously, if she did, she is only using him."

"We're not finished with her. I had never thought I would be dealing with anyone not confronting me about you. I will find her and continue to make her life in turmoil. So much turmoil that she will not be able to take care of her child. Trust me. If Kiara wants to play games, well, let the games begin," Todd declared, forming a devious smile.

Malachi was staring at the ceiling and allowing his thoughts to act as clouds rolling by in the sky. Since school was starting back, Malachi wanted to make many memories with Sakitta as much as possible. The two had been inseparable since playground days. Even both of their grandmothers would tease about them becoming a couple, but Sakitta swore up and down she only cared about Malachi as a friend.

Grabbing his phone, Malachi wasted no time dialing Sakitta's number. "Dear Old Nikki" by Nicki Minaj played as Malachi patiently waited to hear Sakitta's voice.

"Hello," a cheerful voice asked.

"What you up to?" Malachi wondered, for his voice had become thick.

"Boy, don't be trying to smooth talk. What you up to?" Sakitta countered.

"Girl, I asked you first."

"Boy, don't be getting crunk with me. What is it?"

"I was wondering if you would like to spend time with me."

"Where we gonna go?"

"Whatever you want to go?"

"We can't go to Southside. We ain't even ready for that yet."

Although Sakitta was on the other end of the phone, she couldn't see Malachi chuckling. Being around Sakitta was like being around a friend that was always rooting for you. Malachi's feelings for Sakitta were growing stronger every day. Soon, the two will be walking on different paths. Sakitta had aspirations of becoming a registered nurse, but Malachi had aspirations of starting his own car shop. When he wasn't around his friends or Sakitta, Malachi would work at his cousin Antwan's shop. Sometimes, Malachi got paid, but there were times he didn't. He wondered if Sakitta would look at him differently if she found out he was interested in fixing cars. Not too many people saw an interest in wanting to make a living in being a mechanic.

"How about we go to the park and then swing by to grab something to eat?"

"Okay, but don't take me Texas Roadhouse. We ain't ready for that yet," Sakitta stated.

The two decided to take a stroll around Freedom Park. The sun was shining its lovely rays, especially on Sakitta's dark chocolate skin. Kids were running across the field while parents joined in or watched from afar. Some were walking their dogs, while others used the trail to go for a jog. Malachi spotted a bench and made his way toward it. Sakitta plopped right next to him, but she didn't turn to look his way. She could feel his eyes on her, yet Sakitta wasn't so sure why Malachi wasn't looking at the horizon.

"What are you thinking about?" Malachi wondered.

"Can a woman think without being interrupted? Mal, I hate to say this, but your curiosity is similar to a child," Sakitta observed.

"Why are you comparing my curiosity to a child's?"

"Every time we are around each other, you're always asking me a question. I could be wanting to get into my own world, but there you go trespassing with your questions. Shoot. You should have been the one who made *'Asking All Dem Questions.'*"

Malachi let out a slight chuckle. He was definitely going to miss those moments with Sakitta. However, time wasn't a friend on anyone's side, yet Malachi was unsure how to tell Sakitta about his true feelings for her.

"Sakitta, I'm going to be real and honest with you."

"Be honest with me about what?"

This time, Sakitta turned her chocolate eyes toward Malachi. She was indeed skeptical about what he had to say.

"I don't know how or where to begin, but ever since we were kids, I never thought we would last this long. I mean, I don't know how many people that do, but the last thing I ever want is to live a life of regret."

"How?"

"I got feelings for you. I didn't know how to tell you at first. I mean, you're the only girl I see myself with."

Sakitta, at this point, could not find a single word to get out. Never would she ever thought Malachi would possess feelings for her. The two might have been inseparable but becoming more than friends was definitely a challenge. She cherished her friendship with Malachi but moving to the next step was just impossible to her.

"Are you okay?"

"I don't know what to say. We have been rocking since we were in preschool. I mean, I am not trying to end up like Keith and Kiara," Sakitta pointed out.

"Who said we're going to end up like them?" Malachi inquired, expressing a concerned look on his face.

"Look, Mal. You know we look up to them. I mean, I do pray they both find their way back to each other, but like my grandma always says, only God has the last say about everything," Sakitta pointed out.

"True, but at the same time, we can't be comparing ourselves to our friends. Look at them and us, for instance. They go back all the way to diaper days, and we met back in pre-K. They dated all through high school. We ain't even through with high school. They got a kid…"

"And we ain't got no kids. Mal, I don't want to break your heart, but this is something I have to think about. I mean, going from friends to lovers is a big leap. I don't want what we got to go into ruin!"

With no hesitation, Malachi planted a soft kiss on Sakitta's full lips. Sakitta couldn't believe that her own best friend was giving her a lip lock in public. Not wanting to be rude, Sakitta cupped her hands around Malachi's face and kissed him back. Even though Malachi didn't want the kiss to end, air was essential to both of them.

"No matter what you decide, I will always love you. No matter what, I will always love you," Malachi professed, pecking Sakitta on the lips. Both of their foreheads attracted like magnets.

"Girl, why are we here? Heck. This is the last place I want to be at," Amelia protested.

"Girl, I came here to see that officer again. God doesn't make them like He used to. A good bit of them is supposed to be fit like those two officers, but all they want to do is sit behind the desk and smash boxes of doughnuts. Heck, I want those two to feed me some donuts," Stephanie declared.

Amelia couldn't help but giggle at Stephanie. It had been two days since Nuke attacked Amelia, yet Amelia tried her best not to reflect on it. The crew had been sending concerned messages, and Amelia was grateful for it. She never thought in a million years that she would experience a heinous crime from Nuke. He definitely pulled the wool over her chocolate-coated candy eyes.

"Girl, let me go see if they got my restraining order. Don't you get up in here cutting the fool," Amelia demanded.

"Girl, let's go," Stephanie directed, not wasting time to get inside the police station.

Amelia shook her head and hopped out of the car. Migrating to the building, Amelia really wanted to get back inside of her own apartment. Amelia enjoyed the comfort of her home. The only time she went out was if she wanted to go to the bookstore or eat at one of her favorite restaurants. Once both of the friends entered the police station, the police officer behind the desk stood up. He was, of course, heavyset, but the glasses on his face indicated his true age.

"How may I help you ladies today?"

"Excuse me, but have you seen those two fine officers? I promise you, but God doesn't make them like He used to. Where they at?" Stephanie interrogated.

"What fine officers? Girl, you have been watching too many Lifetime movies," the officer objected.

"Look, officer. I just be watching other stuff. Forget Lifetime. They can't even get black stories right. Now, where are those two fine officers at?"

"Look, I don't know which fine officers you are talking about, but if you see them on Lifetime, enjoy watching them."

"Excuse me, officer. You have to look over my friend. I have a question, but is there any update about my restraining order?" Amelia inquired.

"May I have your name, please?"

"Amelia Rucker," Amelia answered.

The police officer began to scavenge through the papers that cluttered on his desk. As Amelia and Stephanie focused on the officer, little did she and Stephanie know that the police officer from the night before made his way toward them. He wasn't with his partner from the night before, but a young man with waves outlined in his hair and Latino bloodline strolled right beside him. The officer recognized Amelia and strolled right to her.

"I never thought I would see you again," he stated.

Immediately, Amelia and Stephanie turned around, but an unusual feeling made Amelia's stomach do flip-flops. She didn't want to rush into another relationship, but there was something about the police officer that made Amelia blush.

"Oh, well. I'm just here to get an update on my restraining order," Amelia replied.

"Where your friend at?" Stephanie butted in.

"Ma'am, last week was his last week."

"Dang, I better tell Kiara then."

"Kiara can't be greedy now. She is either going to play with Samson's dreads or get bent over and handcuffed by the police."

CHAPTER 10

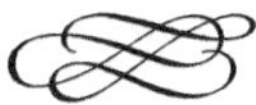

Sakitta was pacing back and forth all because of the scene at the park. She never thought she would hear the word escape from Malachi's mouth. History was one factor, but actions and character proved another factor in how a person felt about another person. *God, what am I going to do?* She thought, pacing, yet her breathing was getting out of control. She grabbed her cell phone and almost dialed Malachi's phone number.

Tossing the phone on the bed, Sakitta let out a shriek. Tears threatened to come down her eyes, and Sakitta soon found herself at the crossroads. Should she just stay friends with Malachi, or was it time to become more?

"Kitta Bug, are you alright?" Grandmother Jean asked.

"Grandma, I don't know what to do," Sakitta answered.

"What you talking about?"

"Malachi confessed his feelings for me. Grandma, Malachi

has been my best friend since playground days. I think what we have is so beautiful, but I don't want it to go to ruin."

"Girl, I knew that boy loved you. Y'all definitely would be cute," Grandma Jean pointed out.

"See, Grandma. You ain't no help." Sakitta pouted.

"Girl, don't make me come back there and snatch all of that hair from your head. You'll be walking around here looking like that doll Angelica had on the *Rugrats.*"

Sakitta couldn't believe that Grandma Jean was adding more to the fury. With no hesitation, Sakitta grabbed her cell phone and dialed Amelia's phone number. "Tears" by Clean Bandit played, and before Louisa Johnson could finish, Amelia answered.

"Hello," she greeted.

"Girl, where you at?" Sakitta wondered.

"Home. Stephanie dragged me to the police station."

"The police station? Girl, what did you do?"

"Kitta Bug, who was at the police station?" Grandma Jean called.

"Grandma Jean, you are so nosy. Stephanie dragged Melia to the police station."

"Kitta, I ain't playing with you about that smart mouth of yours. I can ask now."

"Anyway, Stephanie wanted to go find those fine police officers. So, we only saw one, who is actually the one I like. Don't tell anyone I am about to tell you this, but my stomach did flip flops once I saw him."

"Chocolate or the light-skinned one?"

"The light-skinned one. The chocolate one moved, and guess who apparently had a thang for him," Amelia reported.

"Who?"

"That's why I told your tail to guess."

"Kiara."

"Yes."

"That heifer needs to make her mind up. Whether she is going to try to make it work with Keith or get with the police officer, she can only have one thing inside her at a time."

Amelia burst into giggles. Laughter was pretty much what she needed at the time, especially since she was healing from trauma. Amelia eventually considered Sakitta like a little sister to her. Sakitta basically had not one sibling of her own, but her older cousin, Shagera, was definitely the big sister she really never had.

"Girl, you're crazy," Amelia declared.

"I know, but I'm telling the truth. You can tell she still got a thang for Keith."

"Girl, enough about them. What's on your mind?"

"Girl, Malachi has feelings for me."

"What? Girl, I ain't going to lie to you, but you both will be a cute couple," Amelia pointed out.

"See, you ain't no help either," Sakitta commented.

"Kitta Bug, you and Malachi got history for someone to write a book about. I mean, friends do make the best lovers," Amelia stated.

"That's the thing. What Malachi and I have is so beautiful. A friendship that dates back to playground days and look at us now. I mean, senior year is right around the corner, and he has been my date for homecoming dances, middle school proms, and even junior prom. Now, we're about to enter our last chapter of high school, and the future is definitely unknown.

Don't get me wrong. Mal is fine, but I don't know if we're meant to be."

"That's where you have to pray and ask God if y'all are meant to be. Never try to force anything if it's not meant to be. If it's meant to be, God will allow it. Make sure you take your time and don't try to rush. Love takes time," Amelia ministered.

"Why ain't you a pastor?"

"Sakitta, only God has the last say about everything. I don't want to get up on the pulpit and act the fool. When that time comes, then I will be ready, but God is in control of my life," Amelia declared.

Sakitta sat there, for she allowed the words to marinate her soul. She didn't know whether to become more with Malachi or just remain friends. The only One who could tell her that was indeed God, but how could Sakitta allow God to fix this one?

Kiara was going through the dresses in her closet. A good bit of them only exposed her legs, although they were sculpted with calves. Since she agreed with going to dinner with Keith, Kiara wanted her dress to look as modest as possible. Hopefully, this was just the right step to re-patching their relationship, but Kiara's heart was still covered with scars. She felt like a home wrecker since Todd's wife was the one who answered the phone.

It wasn't long before Kiara came across a black knee length body con dress. It definitely outlined her hips and curves, but Kiara didn't want to give Keith any distractions or naughty thoughts, for that matter. She definitely wasn't the innocent good girl herself, yet she couldn't stop fantasizing about his muscular chest. For some odd reason, Kiara couldn't help but think about feeling safe in Keith's muscular arms. She was definitely traveling back to Memory Lane as sweet moments played in her mind.

Maybe it was a sign for the two to re-patch things up, but Kiara still wasn't ready to open up her heart just yet. Maybe it was all a dream, but was it? The past two nights had brought Kiara to an unfamiliar place. A place where she can feel at ease, a place where she felt secure, and a place that had her on cloud nine.

Knock. Knock. Knock.

The knock at the door immediately brought her back to her reality. Kiara migrated toward the door, but a confused expression formed across her face. She eventually opened the door.

"Look, Ms. Thang. You can't have everything you want," Stephanie stated, barging inside of Kiara's apartment.

"Hold up, Miss Thang. I didn't even invite you inside my apartment. Also, what the heck are you talking about?"

"I dragged Melia to the police station and come to find out Fine Chocolate Officer does not work at the police station. Fine Chocolate Officer is supposed to be mine, and Amelia got a thang for the light-skinned one. I ain't going to lie. Now, he is fine, but that chocolate drop had my name written all over him," Stephanie went off.

"Wait a minute. You dragged Amelia all the way to the police station just to find those two officers?" Kiara quizzed.

"Girl, yes, but don't try to change the subject. How come Melia told me you had a thang for him as well?"

Kiara's eyes grew wide as saucers, for she couldn't believe

Amelia dropped the bomb. She really had not one intention to get with the police officer whatsoever, but it was his dark chocolate skin that allowed her mouth to water.

"First of all, I never said I wanted him. Two. I'm still trying to figure out what I have going on with Keith," Kiara stated in a matter-of-fact tone.

"Well, look. I did not come over here to argue with you. I just came to tell you to make up your mind. You can't be with two men at the same time. Either you're going to be playing with Samson's dreads or get bent over and handcuffed by the po-po," Stephanie stated.

"Stephanie, go home. You're not helping over," Kiara demanded, yet a cramp was being formed in her system due to laughter.

"Alright. Girl, I holla," Stephanie declared, exiting out of Kiara's apartment.

Kiara shook her head at the mess. She wasn't even frustrated or even angry at Amelia. Hopefully, things were slowly healing up for Amelia. The two would definitely chit chat, but Amelia was hardly ever coming over. *I wish something could get done to bring Nuke down. He's still walking the streets.*

She migrated toward the couch and allowed her mind to travel afar.

"Now, ladies, I need your help. Keith is taking me out to dinner, and I have been rambling through my closet trying to find the right dress. I don't want to look like he is trying to take me to a hotel afterward."

It was a peaceful Thursday, and Kiara allowed the girls to come over and assist her with finding the perfect dress. Even Amelia agreed to come over. She was slowly getting back to her usual self, but dating would be on layaway for a minute. Seeing Kiara getting back to wanting to work things out with Keith made Amelia's heart smile.

"Make sure it's not something that is going to give him the idea to drop them drawers after dinner," Stephanie advised.

"Girl, it's only dinner. Besides, Keith and I agreed to take it one day at a time. Besides, y'all can't tell a single soul what I am about to tell y'all, but Keith has hinted about marriage," Kiara disclosed to the girls.

"No," the girls chorused.

"Girl, I missed my boy getting on one bended knee?" Stephanie shrieked.

"Girl, no. He hinted about it to Kyran. Truth be told, I do have so much love for this man, but marriage is a major step. I mean, I still love Keith, but y'all don't know how scared I am," Kiara admitted.

"Trust us. Marriage ain't a fairytale. Imagine being spiritually married to someone you barely even know. I mean, marriage can be spiritual, but I would rather go through the right procedure to become one," Amelia stated.

All eyes immediately turned toward Amelia. *Was she and Nuke spiritually married?* Kiara wondered to herself.

"What do you mean spiritually married?" Bri interrogated.

"Earlier this year, I met a man online. We were talking, but he never once said I was his girlfriend. I was always his wife, according to him. We didn't last because mother was right about him all along. He wanted to use me as a meal ticket," Amelia recalled.

"Hold up. Why didn't you tell us about him?" Stephanie inquired.

"I never considered it real. Anyone that wants to use me is a wolf in sheep's clothing. A husband wouldn't use his wife. He would love and cherish her. I mean, I could see if he was trying to work to meet me halfway, but this man wanted me to pay for him and his son to come live with me. Plus, he had the audacity to disrespect my mom."

"Awe, heck no! Where that fool at?" Stephanie hopped up.

"Stephanie, calm down. This man ain't even worth it. Melia, why didn't you tell us that at one point you were married?"

"Ladies, if I am going to be bonded to someone, then I want to do it legally. I hate to break everyone's heart, but I want to have a godly marriage. The world's view of marriage is fabricated. Not everyone really wants the marriage, but everyone wants a lavishing fairytale wedding," Amelia stated.

"Now, I felt that," Stephanie commented.

"I really did. I really need to decide what I want," Kiara stated.

"Kiara, you and Keith have history like it is no tomorrow. At the end of the day, you can't allow your feelings to dictate your future. Either you're going to be with my boy or you ain't," Stephanie told her.

"Hold up. You might be older than me, but the last time I check, you didn't give birth to me," Kiara shot back.

"Heifer, don't make me snatch all of your hair out of your head. I'm trying to help you out. Keith shouldn't have to suffer from you wrestling with your feelings. As a matter of fact, another man can't love you the same way Keith does," Stephanie retorted.

Kiara couldn't believe the words that came out of Stephanie's mouth. Keith knew exactly what he wanted, and that was to make Kiara his wife. Kiara enjoyed the moments she recently shared with Keith, but were they enough to allow Kiara to change her mind about becoming one with Keith? Sighing, Kiara didn't want to migrate back to the crossroads.

Keith would always text Kiara, sometimes pop up to hang out with her, and cook her favorite entrees. She missed his presence, but most importantly, she missed having him as a shoulder to lean on. Ever since they had gone their separate ways, Kiara would always crawl to her bedroom, especially when she experienced a rough day. Keith was just the type of best friend women should pray to God about. Not a man dipping in and out of their lives. Not a man giving them unrealistic views. Not a man that was treating a woman any type of way, but a man that saw a woman as his better half and companion.

"Are you going to be okay?" Amelia inquired.

"I'm going to be alright, but I don't want to have my hopes crush. I don't want to end up like my mom. I felt she lost her way after my dad passed away," Kiara answered.

"I can relate because, at one point, I was afraid to allow any man to love me the way a man is supposed to love a woman. My mother's first marriage is scarred my heart. Now, whenever I look at her and my father, the love they have for each other is all I really crave for. Is that too much to ask?" Amelia wondered.

"Maybe, I'm afraid to give my heart away," Sakitta admitted.

All eyes immediately were on the young teen girl. Hearing Sakitta admitting what she said had everyone surprised.

"Kitta Bug, you have your whole life ahead of you. Love should be the last thing on your mind. You're about to start senior year. Allow God to send you the right one," Kydra encouraged.

"Tell that to Mal," Sakitta commanded.

"Hold up! Malachi got a thang for you?" Bri shrieked.

"Can y'all calm down? He and I ain't official, but he has told me the L word," Sakitta brought up.

"No?" all the girls chorused.

Sakitta rolled her eyes. She wanted to pinch herself for telling the girls about what Malachi professed to her. Ever since then, Sakitta found herself at a crossroads, for the thin line between friendship and love was indeed a risk. Some couples never went back to friends, especially after a relationship resulted in turmoil.

"At the end of the day, it is about what God says in the end. He is in control of everything. At the end of the day, what do you want?" Kiara questioned.

"I really care about him. Don't get me wrong. All I want is my best friend at the end of the day," Sakitta answered.

That's it! I just want my best friend back. I missed Keith so much that I didn't realize the beauty of friendship. I'm just scared to give my heart back to him. At the end of the day, everything does come between Keith and me. Everything, Kiara thought to herself.

"What is wrong with this dress? Peach is my favorite color," Amelia stated.

"That is why I think you would look perfect in this dress. I mean, peach compliments your skin," Kiara told Amelia.

It was a little after seven that the other girls exited Kiara's apartment. Amelia stayed just a bit longer to assist Kiara with the perfect dress for dinner. Black was what Kiara mainly loved to wear, but Amelia suggested that Kiara try another color.

"Kiara, your hips are more outlined than mine. I mean, we're not the same size," Amelia reminded.

"True, but we're still blessed. This dress is really not my type," Kiara stated, handing Amelia the dress.

Amelia looked at the peach gown and studied it. It was definitely a medium, which was the size for most of her dresses. Tonight, Amelia wanted to focus on her best friend and not herself.

"Well, I can try it once I'm done helping you with finding the right dress," Amelia assured Kiara.

"Great. I still want to wear black."

"Kiara, are you going to a funeral or a hot date?"

"Now, you know black is my signature color. Besides, I should have been the signature model for the little black dress."

"Well, white along with blue, green, orange, and peach is my signature color. Kiara, there is nothing wrong with trying another color. Hey, why not wear purple?"

"Amelia, who in their right mind is going to wear purple? I am not Barney, the dinosaur's daughter."

"Okay. Fine, you win. Black it is," Amelia gave in.

"Also, after we find my dress, I want you to model the dress."

"Kiara, this isn't about me. You are the one going on a date with Keith. I, along with the rest of the crew, will be watching Kyran."

"I get that, but during this time of healing, allow yourself to get dressed up and have a good time. You always used to go out alone before the living ghost, and you became an item."

"True. I can update my wardrobe just by adding another piece."

Both friends looked one time for the dress. Amelia and Kiara both agreed upon a black halter dress that had a ruffle sleeve on the left side. It was right then and there that both girls decided to try the prospective dresses. Kiara was the first one out and waited patiently for Amelia to step out. As soon as Amelia put on the dress, she didn't walk out. She glanced at herself in the mirror as she noticed the dress outlined her figure perfectly. Her dark chocolate skin glowed angelically.

"It's just right," Amelia proudly declared.

She felt the familiar lump struggling her throat. Clenching her fist, Amelia looked up at the ceiling and exhaled. *God, please give me strength.* Amelia silently prayed as she opened the bathroom door and stepped out.

"I told you it would fit. You need to quit doubting yourself whenever something goes wrong. Never allow any man to make you feel worthless because you are definitely a beautiful queen. Matter of fact, we are both queens. Nuke is going to miss out on the wonderful person you are. Men like that don't deserve second chances or good things," Kiara proclaimed.

A tear rolled down Amelia's face, but Kiara wiped it away. The two embraced in a sisterly hug and eventually allowed the tears to fall. Although both women were dealing with different situations, each one had been there for the other. Keith never laid a hand on Kiara, but why did Nuke had to get physical with Amelia?

Love was not gripping a person's wrist hard. Love was not making the other person shed tears at night, and neither was love making a fool out of someone.

CHAPTER 11

"Tiffany, get the door!" Todd instructed from the bedroom.

"Why can't you get the door? I'm trying to get your dinner ready," Tiffany retorted.

Lazy woman. She always wants me to do everything. Todd thought, reluctantly hopping up to get the door. Glancing through the peephole, Todd exhaled a sigh of relief and opened the door.

"Look, we have to come up with a plan to get rid of that heifer. Keith is too good for her," Nuke declared, storming inside of Todd's apartment.

"Look. I might have agreed to work with you, but this is my house. You need to show me some respect," Todd demanded, puffing out his chest.

Nuke had been on the run since he then discovered that the police were looking for him. What many didn't know, especially Kiara and the rest of the crew, was the fact that Todd and Nuke were partners in the black market. Young women, from the ages of eighteen to thirty-three, were slaving and capturing the attention of predators, who were looking to approach and purchase them. Drugs, such as heroine and meth, along with marijuana, flooded the streets, especially in the underground portion of Atlanta.

The swift of steak immediately triggered Nuke's nose. Nuke strolled his way into the kitchen, but he didn't make any sudden moves toward Tiffany. Tiffany didn't bother to look up at Nuke, as she didn't want dinner to be ruin.

"Do you mind if there is room for another?" Nuke inquired.

Tiffany froze. Rolling her eyes, Tiffany remained with her back turned to Nuke. He wasn't the type of person any person would want to call a friend.

"What is it, Nuke? As a matter of fact, what are you doing here?" Her voice was getting heated.

"Awe, Tiffany. I hope you're not upset about what happened three years ago," Nuke brought up.

"Nuke King, you are not the man I thought you were. When you left me on that corner, you fed me to the wolves, allowing those men to do whatever they want to me. Now, I'm married to the man, who eventually brought my freedom. I don't know what to do. Cancer seized my health but torturing young women by thinking Todd actually has a single care in his bone has been wearing me down. Todd and I could have it all, but the road that I have chosen to live has eventually caught up with me. Let this be the last time you step inside of my house," Tiffany warned.

"Tiffany, you can have it all. I mean, you have this nice house. You're married. You're no longer on the corner. As a matter of fact, you have money that is overflowing in your bank account. You have everything that those young women wish they have," Nuke snarled.

Tiffany clenched her fist, for the words that were spitting out of Nuke's mouth were slithering like a serpent. The harsh horrific memories replayed in her mind. The days on the corner made Tiffany feel as if she was trash. Lying in a different bed was not what she expected.

"You've got ten seconds to leave out of my house! Leave before you never walk out of here alive again," Tiffany threatened.

"You're going to need me one day, Tiffany. You're going to need me," Nuke assured in a sly tone.

"Now, Kyran. I want you to behave for everyone. I'm going to pack you your snacks, pajamas, and blanket. Mommy and daddy are going to have a nice dinner. We will get you once we are done with the evening affair," Kiara instructed.

"Is daddy taking you to the club?"

Kiara let out a small giggle. Her party ways were dead and gone, especially now that Kyran was her main priority.

"Daddy is going to take me to dinner. No music scene is a part of the plan. Hopefully, I get to take a nice ride to Southside."

"What is so special about that place?"

"It's a place where you get to star gaze with your date."

"More like the person you love," Kyran corrected.

Kiara did her best to brush off her feelings, but no matter

how hard she tried, the feelings remained on Kiara's mind. She wasn't ready to tell Keith how she felt. Hopefully, dinner was just the step she needed to see where she and Keith should go from there.

"Kyran, only God has the last say about everything. Now, let's get going," Kiara stated.

Both of them exited Kiara's apartment and headed toward Amelia's place. Everyone agreed to be there to assist with Kyran. As soon as they arrived, Kiara texted Keith that she dropped Kyran off. Amelia, along with everyone else, stared in awe of Kiara. The dress, along with her side bun, made Kiara looked extravagant.

Knock! Knock! Knock!

Amelia migrated toward the door and glanced through the peephole. Glancing back at Kiara, Amelia gave her best friend a reassuring smile.

"Your boy is here."

Amelia opened the door and allowed Keith to step inside. Keith modeled a navy-blue Armani suit that outlined his muscular figure. His Calvin Klein cologne made its way into the atmosphere. Kiara's knees buckled, and she couldn't recall the last time besides prom that Keith got dressed up.

"Hey, beautiful," Keith greeted Kiara.

"Hey," Kiara greeted back.

Oh my goodness. I can't believe I am finally going on a date. Kiara thought as she was trying to control her emotions.

"My boy is dressed down to the best. Both of them look as they are going to the BET Awards. Y'all better work it. Now, remember what I always say, Keith. Don't drop the drawers," Tyshon went on.

"Tyshon, gone somewhere. You always saying that," Keith protested.

"Look. I am trying to look after the both of you. Y'all already got Kyran," Tyshon reminded them.

"Trust us. Tyshon, sex is the last thing on Keith's and my mind," Kiara assured.

Everyone was growing irritated of Tyshon's caution message, but Tyshon felt it was best to look after the crew. Tyshon was a year older, along with Stephanie. He was given the nickname Big Brother back in tenth grade, but his brotherly ways were definitely fanatic.

Kiara and Keith scurried out of Amelia's apartment. As they strolled to the car, Keith couldn't help but glance at Kiara. Her golden honey skin was glowing angelically. Kiara did her best to keep her eyes straight ahead, but she glanced back at Keith.

"What is it?" Kiara interrogated.

"I don't know, but you are looking real nice tonight," Keith complimented.

"Thank you. What do you have plan for tonight?"

"Dinner at your favorite restaurant and a ride to Southside. Why?"

"I just wanted to know. It has been forever since a man has taken me out on a date," Kiara answered.

"More like we haven't had a date in forever. So, this is hopefully a start."

Kiara didn't want to show any clues that she was still weighing about the idea of marriage. Granted, having Keith in her life would be dandy, but marriage was not what Kiara wanted to think about. Hopefully, Keith would prove he was the man she would actually spend her life with for eternity.

~

"So, you bring me to my favorite restaurant, and you're not ordering a single thing?" Kiara interrogated.

"I just want to bring you here tonight. Kiara, all I really want to do is spend time with you. I mean, you can ask the server to bring more rolls," Keith answered.

Kiara allowed a burst of giggles to escape. The evening was going too smoothly, but Kiara didn't expect Keith to sit out on a meal. The filet mignon, along with the sautéed shrimp and baked potato, satisfied Kiara, and she thought she was in paradise. Keith's eyes stayed glue on Kiara as if she was the only person in the restaurant.

~

Sitting ten feet from afar, two pairs of envious eyes were on Kiara and Keith. Nuke and Todd could not believe Kiara was sitting and having dinner with Keith. Tiffany didn't accompany the men whatsoever, for Nuke's presence was unsettling for her spirit. Both men immediately kept their eyes on the couple.

"He is really on a date with that harlot. What is it they both see in each other?"

"They're both insane if you ask me. Trust me. It ain't going to last anyway. She's going to get tired of him. I know her. That heifer is too spoiled," Nuke concluded.

"How spoil are we talking here?" Todd wondered.

"Her daddy always took up for her. He was a white man, too."

"What happened to him?"

"The fool croaked over."

Although Todd wasn't aware that Kiara's father was Caucasian, he grew skeptical of Kiara. He always assumed she was just light-skinned, but light-skinned was just a skin tone. She didn't even mention her father to Todd when they first met. *Was her father abusive to her? Did her father abandon her before withdrawing his last breath?*

"Keith, are you okay? You seem like you see someone else is here," Kiara observed.

"I have a funny feeling Nuke is here. Some fool keeps creeping over here as if he is trying to order something but isn't," Keith replied.

Kiara turned to see where Keith was staring at. She couldn't help but feel as if someone was watching over her and Keith, but why would they want to spy on her and Keith? The two just wanted a peaceful evening where they could focus on each other's presence.

"If you want to go, then we can go. See. We should have just skipped the restaurant and rode straight to Southside. I mean, McDonald's would have been alright," Kiara blurted out.

"Kiara, who gets dressed up to go to McDonald's?"

"Church folks."

Keith chuckled at Kiara's answer. Although it was partly true, Keith despised the fact that Kiara's dinner was almost a wreck. As soon as Keith was about to signal the waiter to come over, he caught Nuke red-handed.

"Bingo. I knew it! Stay right here," Keith commanded,

springing up from the table. He migrated toward Nuke, but as soon as he arrived at the table, Keith's eyes grew wide as saucers.

"What's the matter, Keith? Did anyone ever teach you it is impolite to stare at someone?" Todd presented a sly grin on his face.

"Nuke, why are you here with this fool?"

"Look. Who I deal with is none of your concern. Why are you having dinner with that girl? You know my mama don't like that girl," Nuke retorted.

"It doesn't matter what your mama likes. Heck. You ain't the one, who gave her a kid, anyway," Keith shot back.

"Well, that is just too bad," Todd remarked.

Within a flash, Keith yanked Todd by his suit jacket. He clenched his teeth, and his eyes were burning with fire. Todd tried his best to get out of Keith's grip, but Keith's strength was difficult to remove.

"You listen to me. You stay away from Kiara and my child, for if you ever cross paths to get toward them, you're gonna wish you were never born," Keith threatened.

"Keith, let's go! This place ain't getting our business anymore!" Kiara exclaimed, rushing over to Keith's aid.

Kiara's eyes enlarged the minute she rushed over. She couldn't believe Todd was in her sight, but what Kiara felt confused about was that Nuke was sitting across from Todd. *What on earth is going on?*

"Oh, look. If it isn't Miss Thang," Nuke announced.

"Nuke, I knocked your behind out once, and I'll do it again. You got the right one today," Kiara shot back, trying to take off her heel.

"Baby, no. Not today," Keith interjected.

"Kiara, what a shame. Acting unsophisticated in public," Todd commented.

"You lowlife two-timing chump! I wished I never met you," Kiara proclaimed, knocking Todd out the frame.

Immediately, Keith let go of Todd, and swooped Kiara in his arms. Keith didn't expect for dinner to become a segment of *Jerry Springer*. Exiting the restaurant, Keith placed Kiara down as they reached his car.

"Are you mad at me, Keith?" Kiara wondered.

"Why would I?" Keith's chocolate eyes presented a serene expression.

"You told me to stay put, and I hopped up. I didn't want anything to happen to you. Truth be told, police brutality is still on the rise," Kiara explained.

"That showed me you cared. You wanted nothing bad to happen to me, and I felt the same way about you. I'm sorry dinner didn't turn out the way we wanted it to be," Keith apologized.

"Well, before we head to Southside, we should alert Amelia that this fool is still lurking in the streets. Let me call my girl," Kiara stated, taking out her cell phone and headed straight for contacts.

Once she saw Amelia's name, she pressed it and allowed Trin-I-Tee 5:7's "Rescue Me" to play sweetly.

"Hello," Amelia answered.

"Girl, I got some bad news."

"Kiara, what happened this time? What did you do?"

"Girl, calm down. The only thing I did was smack the mess out of Todd."

"Whoa! You saw Todd, and you smacked the fool out of him?"

"Yes. Keith and I can't even sit down to talk and enjoy ourselves. As a matter of fact, Keith didn't even order a thing off the menu. What black person you know goes into a fancy restaurant and does not order a thing off the menu?"

"Don't tell him I am going to say this, but only a slap broke fool will do that," Amelia remarked.

"I am going to let that slide. I hear y'all over there," Keith teased.

Kiara giggled at Keith's statement. She felt relieved knowing that Keith wasn't upset with her. Kiara felt she had to intervene, especially if she didn't want the police to barge inside to detain Keith.

"Anyway, lock the doors. That fool was even out there as well."

"What fool?"

"Nuke. He was sitting at the same table with Todd. I threatened to knock him out as well."

"What is going on? Why are those two hanging out?"

"Who hanging out together?" Tyshon barged in.

"Lawd," Keith complained.

"Todd and Nuke are hanging out. Those two definitely are up to something. Something about this whole situation isn't right."

"Someone go grab Fred and Velma... Hold up. Fred had a thang for Daphne," Tyshon joked.

"Tyshon, shut up. Go to bed or do something," Keith demanded.

"Melia, look. In the meantime, make sure you lock the door,

and you are strapped. If things get out of control, call and let me know ASAP," Kiara instructed.

"Where are y'all heading to tonight?" Tyshon interrogated.

"Southside."

"Southside? Y'all going to be there all night?"

"Tyshon, they are grown. Folks can go to whatever pleases them. Boy, I tell you," Amelia stated, shaking her head.

"Remember what I always. Don't drop the drawers. I don't care how fine she is looking in that dress, but y'all need to wait to break the bed on your honeymoon night," Tyshon recommended.

"Boy, bye. Ain't nobody thinking about getting some. Melia, let us know if Kyran cuts up. We'll be over there in the morning."

"Alright. Y'all be safe. I holla."

"Holla."

Kiara raised her left hand in the air and started to bounce. Keith glanced over at Kiara and let out a chuckle. He turned back his attention back on the road to arrive at their next destination.

"Now, did I just hear that Nuke and Todd were seen at the same place? Something about that whole situation is not sitting right with me," Stephanie analyzed.

"I have to agree. The whole thing is not making sense. Why would Nuke want to hang out with Todd? They barely even know each other," Amelia pointed out.

After getting the whereabouts of Nuke, Amelia still couldn't believe that he was walking in the streets. Nuke wasn't an angel, yet he attacked the woman he claimed he cared about. *Why hadn't the police officer done a thing to find Nuke and place him behind bars?* Amelia wondered. It seemed the police were enabling Nuke to get away with murder scot-free.

"Are you going to be okay?" Bri wondered with concern.

"Yes, but why hasn't Nuke been caught? I don't wish what I had been through on the next queen."

"Look, if he tries anything, y'all just hit up my other crew for the bail money. He has no right to be walking the streets," Kydra proclaimed.

"What other crew you got?" JohnTavis inquired.

"My sister, Bat Bat, and cousin Leondre," Kydra answered.

"Lawd, not Bat Bat. He be the main one ready to fight folks. We should have holla at him to help us against Nuke," JohnTavis stated.

"Lawd, Bat is going to have us all thrown in jail. Ain't this a mess," Tyshon chimed in, throwing up his hands.

As soon as Tyshon flopped on the couch, Malachi and Sakitta's voices raised the hair on the backs of everyone's necks. Kyran was sleeping in Amelia's room, but the two friends were right across from it. Everyone immediately tiptoed to see what was going on between the two teens.

"Mal, that is your problem. You're not being patient with me. You're not allowing me to think things through. You're the one impatient," Sakitta shot back.

"Sakitta, the only thing I have done is asked you have you decided yet. I'm not mad. I just wanna know," Malachi stated.

"How can we become more than friends if you don't have patience with me? Every time we're around each other, you be like, 'Kitta, have you made a decision yet'?" Sakitta imitated Malachi.

"I hate to ask, but be patient about what?" Tyshon wondered.

"He has feelings for her," Amelia answered.

"We all knew that. They be around each other all the time," JohnTavis pointed out.

"Donnie McClurkin, it is a blessing that you even realize it," Tyshon commented.

"Look. Don't y'all start that mess," Amelia demanded.

"You know what, Kitta? I'm out. You're tripping," Malachi stated.

He opened the door, but before he could head to the front door, Tyshon grabbed Malachi by his arm. A tear threatened to fall down his gorgeous face, but Sakitta rushed out of the room and raised her in the air.

"Sakitta, no, no!" JohnTavis demanded.

"I'm sick of him! I don't even want to see you again!" Sakitta proclaimed, choking on the lump inside of her throat.

"Look. All of y'all are about to raise up out of here! Kyran is asleep. As a matter of fact, everybody head to bed. We will handle this in the morning," Amelia went off on her friends.

"Hold up. Where are we all going to sleep at?"

"Boys, sleep in the empty room. Ladies, come to my room," Amelia directed.

"Man, I was just about to head to my grandma's house," Malachi complained.

"Well, look. Keith is gone probably talk some sense into you."

"He got his own problems."

"Shut up, boy," Amelia warned, heading straight for bed.

CHAPTER 12

"Tell me what's on your mind," Keith requested.

"The fact that I never thought I would be sitting in your car and stargazing. I don't remember the last time I was even at Southside. I mean, this is definitely a romantic spot," Kiara stated.

Although she didn't get the chance to finish her entire dinner, Kiara brushed the scene out of her head. She still couldn't get over the fact that Todd and Nuke were sitting in the same area. Kiara allowed her mind to wander afar as she focused more on the present. She never thought she would be alone at this very moment with Keith.

"I know there is probably something else on your mind," Keith observed. His eyes stayed glued on Kiara.

"I mean, I didn't expect to be alone with you. Kyran's not here to calm down my nerves. I mean, the truth is we're not official."

"But we're working on us."

"I get it, but the last thing I want to do is hurt you."

"How are you going to hurt me? I hate to bring this up, but when I stormed out of your place, I really hurt you," Keith admitted, trying his best not to reflect on the past.

"I don't want to get your hopes up. Keith, I'm still trying to heal, and grant it, I got my best friend back...."

"I want to come home to my best friend every day. You don't know how much I hate being in my apartment alone because I don't have you and Kyran in my presence. That is what I really want. I want to become a family with you and Kyran. We ain't going to be shacking in. I want you to be my wife," Keith professed.

"Keith, I know you want to be married. Heck, I want to be married, too, but..." Kiara choked, for if the words spat out of her mouth, then the whole evening would go up in flames. She felt she had to be honest with Keith about how she really felt. If she and Keith were to become one and they experienced another argument, nine out of ten, the marriage would go up into flames.

Trying her best to control her emotions, Kiara inhaled and exhaled. Keith reached over and grabbed her hand.

Chocolate eyes stared at one another, yet the two individuals forgot they were no longer secured behind closed doors. They were surrounded by stars that provided them with an illuminated view in hopes that a shooting star will appear. An owl hooted, alerting the two of its presence. Crickets and frogs chorused in unison, for the two species were far apart from one another.

"Tell me," Keith directed gently.

"Tell you what?"

"What are you afraid of? I know you, and when something is bothering you, you tense up. You can be honest with me, KiKi," Keith assured.

"I… Keith, I just want to take my time with you. I mean, to be real, I just slowly allowed you back into my life. I want to see where this is going to take us."

"Have I forced you to do anything that you don't want to do?"

"No. You're probably what every woman wishes the man in her life was. You didn't even force me to open my legs to you. I mean, we both got caught up in the moment."

"True that."

Kiara did not want to take the slow ride back to Memory Lane, so she quickly dismissed the moment. She wished she had the strength to be real with Keith, but the words were playing tug of war with her heart. The crossroads definitely felt more like her new residence since she seemed to never mentally exit from there.

"So, do you want to head back or camp out here tonight?"

Kiara's nose scrunched up.

"Boy, I'm in a dress and some high heels. If I had known that you were planning to take me camping, I wouldn't have come like this," Kiara retorted, controlling her tone.

"You never slept in the car while stargazing at Southside. Heck, I did this with Unc one time, and my goal is to do the same with you and Kyran. Stuff like that matters to me. Forget the matching outfits, expensive dates, and all of that other stuff that social media feeds into the minds of young, naive girls and boys. I want to make memories by enjoying the simple things in life," Keith explained.

Kiara's eyes enlarged. The words that escaped from Keith definitely made Kiara's heart smile, yet she was doing everything in her power to control hers.

"Did you bring a blanket?" Kiara inquired.

Keith unbuttoned his shirt, but Kiara's eyes immediately enlarged. Keith was trying to have a romantic evening at Southside, but this wasn't how she intended for it to be.

"Keith, are you trying to give the wildlife a show? I mean, first, you want to spend the night in the car, and now, you're taking off your shirt because you ain't got no blanket," Kiara went off.

"I'm trying to give you my shirt, so that way you can be warm. I got a shirt underneath. Girl, it ain't like the animals can throw some ones at me," Keith stated.

He continued to unbutton his shirt, and once he completed the task, he removed it and handed it to Kiara. She placed it on and placed her head on Keith's shoulder. Keith embraced his muscular arms around Kiara, but before he allowed his eyes to roll in the back of his head, Keith planted a kiss on Kiara's forehead.

"Good night, beautiful," Keith stated.

"We gotta get rid of both of them. Keith can come last, but Kiara is the main issue. We have to get rid of her ASAP!" Nuke exclaimed, as his blood level reached its boiling point.

"Look. You can handle Keith. That is your own blood. Kiara is my problem, so I can handle her," Todd assured Nuke.

After the fiasco at the restaurant, Todd and Nuke were

ready to plot plan B. Kiara and Keith might have won the battle, but the war was far from complete. Now, it was time to let Keith and Kiara know who the big dogs were around Atlanta.

"Keith is your kin," Todd reminded Nuke.

"That doesn't mean I like him," Nuke retorted.

Nuke always couldn't stand the presence of Keith. Ever since they were young, Nuke always wanted to be the one who excelled at everything. School definitely wasn't Nuke's greatest area of performance. Keith would get highlighted in the local newspaper and receive academic honors as well. Nuke forfeited school, for the street life was his place of duty. The street life provided Nuke the credentials he always strived for. The feds hunted him down like a deer in the forest, but Nuke managed to dodge the bullets.

"Look. We both got pests that we have to deal with, and like pest control, we got to exterminate them," Todd professed, raising his hands in the air.

"Look. We are going to handle them one at a time," Nuke reinforced.

Tiffany couldn't believe how ignorant the two men were going on. Going along with their plans was like working the graveyard shift. Her body wasn't like a twenty-one-year-old, where it would store all the energy she needed. Todd hardly catered to her own needs, yet they barely consummated after tying the knot. Tiffany even wondered was the whole marriage concept even necessary. Tormenting young females with Todd was one thing, but uniting as a spouse, where there was no satisfaction, was a different type of hell.

I have to do something. I can't keep allowing these two to get away with all of this mayhem. I am worn out. I want to be emancipated.

God, what am I going to do? She thought as a familiar lump strangled her throat.

Nuke noticed Tiffany not breathing a single word. He
strolled toward her, but the minute she caught Nuke in motion,
he froze.

"I just want to ensure you are wide awake. You haven't been
cooperating much," Nuke stated slyly.

"Don't you and Todd ever get tired of wanting to always
harm an innocent bystander? I don't see how people like you
have breath in your body and still carry on doing the devil's
work. Don't you get tired of living in sin?" Tiffany challenged.

"You ain't no saint. Since when did you become Mother
Teresa? You might as well get that mentality out of your head,"
Nuke shot back.

Tiffany exhaled, for a meeting with her fists and Nuke's face
would liberate some of her tension. Tiffany prayed that there
was something better than harming other people, who had not
one ounce of scheming to torture her in the first place. Tiffany
longed for an environment where she wouldn't toss and turn
every night and live far from men like Nuke and Todd.

"So, how was your first night in Southside?" Keith wondered.

"Okay. Why didn't you tell me you enjoyed stuff like this?"

Kiara took off Keith's shirt and handed it back to him. Keith
took it back, but he stayed glued to the beauty sitting on the
passenger side. Kiara's beauty hypnotized Keith, and he thought
it was unnecessary for her to mask it with any cosmetic.

"I told you last night. I am all for making memories, not

investing money into things I will eventually toss out. Sometimes, you have to think of what really matters instead of what social media uses as propaganda. Making memories is priceless. Baby girl, you can't always get priceless moments back."

"What happened to the Keith I went to high school with?"

"He became a father. He had to evolve into a man quickly. His views on life metamorphosed into something that can't be explained. Why?"

"Well, I never thought that you would say anything like that. I mean, you must have done something in order to really change," Kiara stated.

"It's all about mindset. You have to look at life from a certain perspective — what matters versus what doesn't matter. Smaller things will always have a bigger impact in life. Why? You shall always strive to cherish the smaller things and moments in life. For instance, we slept underneath the stars. I will always cherish this moment.

Kiara allowed the words to marinate her soul. She really hadn't thought about how much this date really meant to Keith. She never even once considered how much this date actually meant to her. Kyran never made a fuss about his mother being out, for his only hope was for his parents to be together.

"You gonna be good?" Keith inquired.

"Yeah. I'm going to be good. I'm just ready to get out of this dress and don't even think about giving me a sly smile, mister," Kiara directed.

"What sly look? Girl, you're over here telling on yourself. I'm ready to get back to my spot. Hopefully, I can get a kiss before we head back," Keith requested.

With no hesitation, Kiara leaned toward Keith, and their lips met in a sweet kiss. Keith cupped both of his hands around Kiara's face. Their tongues twirled with one another, yet their familiar greeting was always unexpected. Their lips broke apart, but Kiara sensed an ache for more. Steering Keith in the wrong could jeopardize what they were building. *Why am I afraid to open up to Keith? I mean, I could see if Keith raised his hands at me and used me like a punching bag. I could see if Keith called me everything but a child of God. I could see if Keith made up so many lies that could actually give him a spot on the spot on the New York Times Bestsellers. God, what is wrong with me?* She thought, fighting with the various thoughts flashing in her mind.

"You good?" Keith quizzed.

"Yes. I'm going to be good. Can you get us out of here, please?"

"Say less."

Keith put the key into the ignition and drove straight to Kiara's apartment. They quickly glanced at one another from time to time, and not a word escaped from either one.

"Look. Y'all are both young, and if it's meant for you both to be together, then God would allow it. Heck. You both need to start putting your trust in God," Amelia ministered to Sakitta and Malachi.

"You don't ever get tired of preaching to us, huh?" Malachi wondered.

"Boy, my mouth might go dry, but I don't get tired. I am on a mission for God. Too many souls leave this earth without Jesus, and Hell's belly keeps getting bigger and bigger. I am not ashamed of the Gospel, and the words that will come out of my mouth will be sound doctrine and not anything that will lead others astray. Too many false prophets have gone out into this world and deceived too many in the flock. We don't know what's real and what's fake anymore," Amelia explained.

"Can I get an amen?" JohnTavis jumped up.

"Donnie McClurkin, please sit your tail down," Tyshon demanded.

The hour hand stretched at eleven while the minute hand was on the twelve. Sakitta sat with Amelia, as her eyes never took the risk to notice Malachi. Malachi's blood level rose like the red needle in a thermometer. He was aware that time was indeed an enemy and not a loyal friend. He yearned for her touch and full lips to devour. Malachi visioned a future with Sakitta, where they would come home to a cozy house after a long day at work. Different entrees would hit the spot since both of their ethnicities never originated from America.

Not a single word escaped from anyone. Kyran was in Amelia's bedroom, where he watched *Paw Patrol*.

Dang. Can someone break the silence in here? I feel like we're in an asylum, JohnTavis thought.

"That's it! I've had enough!" Malachi stood up and raced toward the door.

"It's about time somebody said something up in here. I felt like we were in a cemetery," JohnTavis commented.

"Donnie McClurkin, you had to say something after this boy opened his mouth," Tyshon chimed in.

"Where are you going?" Amelia questioned.

"I'll beat my grandma's house."

As soon as Malachi opened the door, he didn't even acknowledge Kiara and Keith's presence. Frowns formed across their faces, yet the couple turned their attention to everyone.

"What's wrong with that boy?" Keith inquired.

"He and Kitta Bug got into it," Amelia answered.

"Kitta Bug, he didn't hit you, did he?"

Before Sakitta could give Keith the truth, Malachi charged at Keith. Huffing and puffing, he clenched his fist.

"Why you ask her that?"

"Hold up, boy." Keith turned around to face Malachi.

"Y'all, they fighting!" JohnTavis announced.

Everyone, including Amelia, rushed toward the door. Kiara pulled Keith away so that he wouldn't perform any damages toward Malachi.

"You need to be worrying about how you're going to repair your broken relationship," Malachi shot back.

"Hold up. What you ain't going to do is bring my relationship in this. I have every right to ask Sakitta that. We still got a fool that is on the loose for putting his hands on one of our friends. So, yes, I'm going to ask," Keith retorted.

Amelia migrated back into the kitchen and opened the cabinet. She scavenged through her pan until she came across a pan black as coal that depicted scales as if a forty-niner had used it in search of gold. Rushing back toward the door, Amelia showcased the iron skillet. Everyone's eyes enlarged as soon as the iron skillet was present.

"Melia, what are you about to do with that?" Stephanie wondered.

"Knock the devil out of this boy if he tries anything," Amelia answered.

"Instead of knocking me out, you should have knocked Nuke out instead," Malachi remarked.

"That's it!" Amelia charged toward Malachi as the skillet rose high in the air.

"No, Melia! No!" Everyone protested.

"Look. Until you act right, don't come around here anymore. And yes. I am telling your grandma on you," Keith went off.

Turning away, Malachi strolled out of the hallway. Everyone migrated back inside Amelia's apartment. Closing and securing the door, all eyes were on Sakitta. Amelia still had the iron skillet, but Sakitta was her main focus.

"Now, before we were rudely interrupted by that fool, you never did give us an answer. Now before you give me an answer, what happened?" Keith interrogated.

"Boy, you sound like a pastor that does not know which sermon to preach," Tyshon blurted.

"Boy, this is a time to get serious. We can't have young men in our group that are putting paws on women. We can't be having that. Not up in here we ain't," Keith responded.

"Alright, Keith!" Amelia stated, raising her tone.

"Malachi professed his love toward me last week. I told him I would think about it. Y'all know me and that boy got history," Sakitta reminded them.

"Girl, history does not mean a thing, especially if he ain't treating you right," Tyshon declared.

"That part. Mhmm," Keith agreed, bouncing his shoulders up and down.

"Every day I kept getting text messages asking if I made up my mind about what he asked me. Y'all don't know but having second thoughts can really weigh you down. I still don't know, and then last night, he pushed me. I can't think or focus on my goals without a millisecond of him asking if I made up my mind."

"That is a red flag right there. If a man can't be patient with you, then he doesn't deserve your heart. You deserve better if you ask me," Keith stated.

As Sakitta allowed the words to marinate her soul, she tried her best to keep her composure. The way Malachi reacted toward her was indeed a real-life moment. Thankfully, he didn't put his hands on her, but if he was going to throw temper tantrums like a four-year-old, then what was the use of actually being in a fully committed relationship with him?

Everyone stayed for another hour or two. Sakitta ensured she would be cool, so there was no need to come over to her grandmother's place. Before Keith and Kiara could exit the place, Amelia giggled as both of her friends froze and stared at her.

"What?" Keith wondered.

"Y'all are forgetting someone," Amelia told them.

"Whoo! My baby! Where is he?" Kiara tried to catch her breath, for her heart was racing.

"He is in my room. He's quiet. Again, Kyran didn't give me any trouble."

As Amelia kept yapping, Kiara raced to the bedroom. Once getting there, Kiara let out a sigh. Kyran was slumbering like an angel. Kiara tiptoed and picked up her son, and his eyes crept open for a second.

"Mommy, where's daddy?" Kyran interrogated, yet his eyes were still closed.

"Daddy is here. He is waiting on us."

Kiara migrated back to where Amelia and Keith were. She gave Keith Kyran to hold while she headed back to grab his tablet and shoes. As soon as Kiara made her way back, Kiara hugged Amelia before she and Keith exit the apartment. As they both walked side by side, Keith glanced over at Kiara, who kept her eyes straight ahead. A genuine smile formed across his handsome face. Kiara's radiant beauty was making his heart do a skip run. He felt he hit the jackpot having the two important people in his life by his side.

God, let everything be done in thy will. Keith silently prayed.

CHAPTER 13

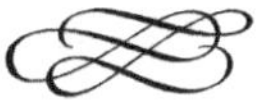

"Look. We have to get in full motive. We have to get rid full of that little tramp once and for all. Keith deserves someone better than that thang anyway," Nuke ranted.

Blue Flame was like an arena on Saturday Night. Ballers and shot callers ensured their wallets were stuffed to tip or make it rain on the exotic dancers. Women, especially fresh out of high school, were scavenging in hopes of scoring a baller for the night. Nuke and Todd were in the back of the club. This time, both men were ready to go all in on how to get rid of Kiara once and for all.

Tiffany decided to make an appearance at Blue Flame. Todd didn't know why Tiffany was acting strange, but soon, everything will come shining in the light.

"Nuke, we have to stay alert at all times. You're more excited than I am. Heck. She has to come around, but eventually, we will be ready," Todd stated.

Not once was Todd's or Nuke's heart doing a 360. Todd had been making false hopes and promises for years. He simply enjoyed every moment of it, and not a single moment of remorse would come to his mind. This was pretty much like an extracurricular activity.

"Pretty soon, friend, the entire city of Atlanta will be feared by the both of us. At the end of the day, no one will conquer in putting an end to us," Todd snarled.

"Look, I'm going to keep it straight one hundred with you, so don't take it personally. We are not Tommy and Ghost, so don't think we're partners in crime as well. We're here to manipulate and yet conquer. Money is our motive at the end of the day. These young harlots will soon be working on the corner, and until they make a dime, they won't come off. Atlanta will be the New Jack City. Goodbye to becoming the New Hollywood," Nuke performed.

Not a word escaped Todd, yet the crooked smile plastered all over his face. Nuke and Todd basically never had a guys' night out, for everything was strictly business between the two.

"Nuke, in this game, there is definitely no room for friendship. Remember, it gets lonely at the top of the pyramid. We're both in this race to climb the pyramid, but only one of us can conquer the world," Todd snarled.

Chocolate but fiery eyes glared at blue oceanic eyes. Not a bond made these two tight like glue. Not even a word of encouragement was exchanged between them. Pretty soon, the race to conquering the world was ticking like a bomb. Only one man would prevail, while the other one will allow his pride to be his downfall.

"Kitta Bug, you have been quiet for the past few weeks. Is everything going good?" Jean wondered.

"Grandma, all I care about at the moment are my goals. I don't need anyone distracting me from becoming a nurse," Sakitta answered.

She scrolled through her Facebook timeline, yet the group was barely on. Sakitta didn't hear a peek even from Malachi, and she had grown fond of not hearing a single question come out of his mouth, yet his presence made her yearn for him. She didn't want to admit it, but no matter how hard Sakitta tried to erase the thought and image of Malachi, it was as if the thought and image of him prevailed.

"Sakitta, I am so glad that you want to stay focus on your goals. That's what you need to be doing, anyway. Wood comes a dime a dozen," Jean reminded Sakitta.

"Grandma, who said anything about chopping wood?"

"Kitta, I ain't talking about that wood. Girl, you are something else. You know good and well what I'm talking about — the head between a man's leg. He thinks more with that than the head on his shoulder," Jean went on.

Once Sakitta caught on to what her grandmother was saying, she shook her head. Sex was the least thing on her mind. She wanted to stand with the man God appointed as her husband and unite as one. Then, on the honeymoon night, breaking the bed was going to be in full action.

Knock. Knock. Knock.

Who is this? She thought, remaining in her seat.

"Girl, I know you heard that knock at the door. Go open the door," Jean commanded.

Sakitta stomped toward the door. She felt unenthusiastic about seeing anyone. Everything was serene until the person at the door interrupted her moment.

"Sakitta, you better fix your attitude before I fix it for you. Walk like you got some sense," Jean warned.

Sakitta quickly stepped from stomping to a calmer migration. Without looking through the peephole, Sakitta opened the door, and her eyes grew wide as saucers. A genuine smile formed across Malachi's face. A rose like Snow White's lips was presented in his right hand.

What now? Sakitta thought, pinching herself.

"Hey, Sakitta," Malachi greeted.

Slam!

Of all days, this fool wants to show up. Sakitta thought, poking out her lips.

"Sakitta, if you don't open that doggone door, I know something," Jean warned.

"Grandma, Malachi is the last person I want to see. The boy is too impatient, and the last thing I need is to be tied to someone impatient. I was doing fine without him the last couple of weeks. I will be fine without him forever more," Sakitta defended.

"Your heart is telling you one thing, yet the way you are going on is telling a whole different story. Sakitta, for you and Malachi to have a strong relationship, you both need to have Jesus in the center of it. Y'all young folks need to stop looking at what's on reality shows and social media for relationship goals. Most of those folks are not happy in real life. All of that is false hope," Jean lectured.

"I don't want to see him. I don't want to see him," Sakitta whined.

"I get that. You need to tell him that yourself. Heck. You have to see me every day whether you like it or not. I'm the one taking care of you. Sakitta, if Malachi can't respect your wishes, then what is the point of having him in your life. You need to put your foot down and set your boundaries."

Without hesitation, Sakitta migrated outside. Malachi followed her, yet Sakitta didn't notice.

"Sakitta," Malachi called.

"What, Mal?" Sakitta turned around, not smiling.

"Can we talk?"

"Oh. You got that right. I want you to listen to me, and you better hear me out. I have dreams, and I have goals, and at the end of the day, I will accomplish them with or without you. Look, I still haven't decided on becoming more than friends because the last thing I need is any distraction."

"Look. I don't know how you will take this, but these past couple of weeks have me about to go insane in the membrane. I missed your presence. I mean, I miss hearing your voice. I miss holding your hand. I miss making you laugh. I miss you whenever you cross my mind. You have to look over me. I get too attached because, at the end of the day, you're the one that I want. The only one I want," Malachi professed.

Sakitta froze. The words that spat out of Malachi's mouth ran like arrows in her mind. Malachi migrated toward Sakitta as their chocolate eyes gazed into one another. Malachi extended out the rose, and Sakitta accepted it, although no words escape from her mouth. Malachi planted a lingering kiss on her forehead.

God, what am I going to do? She thought, allowing her mind to wander to the other side of town.

~

"So, what are you thinking of?" Keith wondered.

"Nothing much. What are you up to, mister?" Kiara inquired, biting her lips. She fought the bashfulness that tried to appear on her face.

"Why do you think I always got to be up to something?"

"Because at the end of the day, I know you. You almost sneak attacked me at my place. Plus, you got jealous when I said the police officer was fine. Obviously, he was, but that doesn't mean I want him," Kiara told Keith.

The past two weeks were fresh beginnings. Both Kiara and Keith focused more on Kyran as a team but even focused on each other more. The two would take walks through the park and even enjoy having dinner at each other's apartment. Today, both just wanted to be in each other's presence. Kyran glued his eyes to *The Lion Guard*.

"Well, you were going on bad about him while you were right in front of me."

"Boy, I don't know anything about him. As a matter of fact, I hope Stephanie caught up with him," Kiara stated.

Keith chuckled at Kiara's answer. Since it has only been him and Kiara lately, the gang seemed to be too tied up in their own affair. Kiara knew how essential that space was for her friends as well. Especially since she and Keith were working on their relationship, Kiara realized this was not a matter of playing around. This very moment and time could determine how her relationship could be affected.

Keith reached over and entwined his hand with Kiara's. Her chocolate eyes soon turned to stare deeply into his. It wasn't often that two would allow their hands to meet and greet, but something about this very moment allowed Kiara to feel the butterflies from inside of her.

"You good?" Keith wondered.

"Yes. Why do you ask?"

"I can't ask my girl anything. What type of man would I be if I didn't?"

"I mean, I ain't going to trip, but it has been a minute since we held hands."

Keith caressed Kiara's left ring finger, which made Kiara turn her attention to the massage. *Why was Keith massaging my finger? It wasn't as if he noticed it like last week.*

Kiara turned her attention toward the wall as her mind began to allow so many thoughts and questions to taunt her. *What if Keith proposes? You're not ready to be a wife. You'll be stuck as a baby mama. It won't last. You're both too young. Look at your parents. Their marriage didn't last long.*

"Kiara, are you okay?" Keith broke Kiara out of her trance.

"Keith, I have to go. Look. Just bring Kyran over once you are done," Kiara announced, hopping up and migrating toward the door.

Dang. What's wrong with shawty? Keith wondered, expressing a concerned look.

Kiara opened the door, and the moment she stepped

outside, a masked figure grabbed her. He covered her mouth, but Kiara had sunken her teeth into his hand.

"Ow!"

"Help! Help!" Kiara cried.

"Nobody is going to help you! You will be gone forever, you little harlot," a second masked figure stated.

"Keith! Keith!"

Keith raced toward the door, but the moment he had gotten there, the kidnappers took off with Kiara.

Snap! What am I going to do? Keith thought, punching the door.

Time wasn't on anyone's side, and Keith knew he had to get to Kiara before the kidnappers did any serious damage to Kiara. He flew inside of his apartment and grabbed Kyran.

"Daddy, what's going on?" Kyran wondered for he thought his father was going to twirl him around.

"I'll explain everything to you later. Your grandmother is going to have to look after you. Daddy has some business to handle," Keith explained.

Keith checked his pocket and raced right back toward his apartment. He migrated toward his room and seized the keys along with his cell phone and the burgundy velvet box. Kyran kept his eyes forward, but he still wondered what was going on.

As soon as Keith approached his car, he took out his keys to unlock the door. He fastened Kyran in his booster seat and then jumped inside of the driver's seat. Putting the keys into the ignition, Keith sped out of the parking out. Keith knew he had to find Kiara immediately, but where on earth could the kidnappers have taken her?

Keith pulled up to a small brick house and honked the horn. A medium-sized lady rushed out of the house to see who alerted her. Her satin bonnet protected her curls, which were rolled up in cotton candy and mint green hair rollers. Her skin was smooth as dark chocolate, yet not a single wrinkle was drawn on her face.

"Keith, what's wrong with you? I'm over here trying to get ready for my date," Keith's mama ranted.

"Mama, you always out with a different man," Keith commented.

"At least they are not getting inside my oven the same way you got inside of Kiara's. As a matter of fact, where that girl at?" she wondered, noticing Kiara wasn't in the car.

"Mama, she's been kidnapped. Please watch Kyran for me while I go get her back."

"Kidnapped? You better be glad that her folks ain't here, both of her grandmothers, along with that fine granddaddy of hers. Child, if he was still alive and not with Sara, I'll jack him up so fast…"

"Mama, stop being nasty now! Were you really going to do that?" Keith expressed a funny expression on his face.

"Boy, yeah. Everything underneath here is not Victoria Secret," she added.

"Mama! Look, ma. I ain't got time to hear your fantasy. Go listen to Ludacris. I need to find Kiara so that I can get her back to safety. I need you to watch Kyran as I go ahead and do this. Please," Keith pleaded.

"Okay. I can cancel my date but hear me out. When you find

her, don't drop those drawers. You already got Kyran. I love my grandson, but if you and Kiara want to multiply, become one in the sight of the Lord," Keith's mother ministered.

"Mama, you sound like everyone else."

"Because I am speaking the truth. A real mother will always want better for her children. I ain't going to lie, but I'm glad you never turned out to be anything like your father. That fool traded you in for alcohol. The streets were his place of duty."

Keith never resented his father, but his father's absence motivated him to be a better man and father toward his own child. Now wasn't a time to travel back to Memory Lane, but his mother's encouraging words of making Kiara his wife were essential.

Keith put the car in park, but he kept the door open and raced to the other side. He opened the door and unstrapped Kyran out of his booster seat and took him out. Before heading back to his car, Keith kneeled in front of Kyran and pressed his forehead against his.

"Daddy is going to go find mommy and bring her back. I want you to behave for grandma. I will be back, and mommy will be back as well. Okay? "

"Yes, sir," Kyran stated.

Keith embraced Kyran in a fatherly hug. A tear threatened to fall down Keith's face. Keith started to migrate back toward his car.

"Keith, if you ain't back here by nine o'clock, I am calling the police and the insurance man," his mother told him.

"You got insurance on my daddy?" Kyran wondered.

"Boy, gone get inside of the house. You stay out of grown people's business," Keith's mama demanded.

Keith chuckled at the moment between his mother and Kyran. As soon as he hopped back inside of the car, Keith took out his cell phone and dialed the group chat's number for a video call. Pretty soon, everyone joined and was astonished to see Keith.

"'Bout time we heard from you, boss man," Malachi blurted.

"Where's Kiara?" Amelia wondered.

"That's why I'm calling you. She has been kidnapped," Keith informed.

"Kidnapped?!" Everyone chorused.

"We gotta save her right this minute!" Tyshon hopped up and threw his hand up in the air.

"Hold up! My question is who has Kiara?" Amelia interjected.

"Girl, it has to be Todd. This has his name written all over. We gotta go find her," JohnTavis chimed in.

"Y'all still have your camouflage outfits?"

"Heck yeah. We knew we might need them again," Stephanie stated.

"Good. Wear those and bring those baseball bats. Melia, bring the iron skillet. Look. Everyone is going to have to carpool," Keith instructed.

"You ain't gotta tell us twice. As a matter of fact, hide your kids. Hide your wives. Hide your husbands because they are kidnapping everybody out here," Tyshon exaggerated.

"Alright, y'all! Dang! We have to find Kiara!"

"Where is she at?" Bri shrieked in a high-pitched voice.

"She might be at Blue Flame," Sakitta pointed out.

"Now, Sakitta, you know good and well you can't take your tail to Blue Flame," JohnTavis reminded her.

"Shoot. Her body says otherwise," Malachi pointed out.

"Mal, if you want to keep your eyes and soul, I suggest that you keep your thoughts to yourself," Sakitta warned.

"Whoo! Somebody is feisty," Malachi teased.

"Alright, Bobby and Whitney! The more we sit here and not move, we're allowing the enemy to have their moment with harming Kiara. Now, let's put our differences aside and get our girl back!" Kydra declared.

"Alright now. Y'all got Kydra turnt!" Keith declared.

Click!

Keith knew he had to head over to Blue Flame immediately. Although the party scene never caught his attention, Keith couldn't get over the fact Kiara might be hidden at the club. *Why was Todd even at Blue Flame? Does he know Pastor Troy made a song about the infamous club?* Keith thought, trying to piece the puzzles together.

As soon as he was five minutes away from Blue Flame, Keith said a quick prayer to the Almighty.

Heavenly Father,

As my friends and I go through the valley of darkness, protect us and please allow us to come out of the valley the same way we walked in. Most importantly, please watch over the woman I love. Lord, if it's meant for her to be my wife, let everything be done in thy will and not my way. I love her so much. I can't lose her. Amen.

A tear escaped, yet Keith pulled his strength together.

As soon as he pulled up to Blue Flame, Keith parked his car and hopped out. He searched for the rest of the crew and waited until they showed up. As soon as he heard Pastor Troy's "No More Play in GA," Keith noticed the rest of the gang pulling up. As soon as Amelia turned off the song, Tyshon hopped out of the car and still got hyped, as if the music was still playing.

"We ready! We ready! We ready!"

"Tyshon, calm your tail down! The song is gone," Keith stated.

"Shoot. Melia was the one who played it. We were turnt coming over here!" Tyshon declared.

"Alright. Since we're all here, how are we going to run up in there?" Stephanie wondered.

"Dang. How are we gonna roll up in there?"

"Follow me. I gotta plan," Keith stated.

Everyone else followed Keith to the front of the club. As soon as everyone made his or her way inside the club, the club wasn't packed to their surprise. A young bartender noticed the gang, but she immediately turned back to washing cups.

"Something is different," Tyshon blurted out.

"Tyshon!" everyone chorused.

CHAPTER 14

"Well, well, well. Look who we have here," Nuke snarled.

"Let me go!" Kiara demanded.

"No. That won't be an option. You see, Kiara, my main mission is to cause pain to women like you. You were too blind to see that there was not a single sign of a beautiful future. I wasn't Prince Charming, but to be real, Prince Charming only exists in fairytales. I never went on a single date with you, held your hand, kissed your forehead, or any of that matter.

Yes, I'm married, but that doesn't mean my wife satisfies me. Cancer robbed her of her beauty, yet she was in the plot, too. We have caused more damage internally than we have externally. Our goal was to make you forget about Keith," Todd explained.

"Keith will always be a better man than any of you scumbags. Nuke, you put your hands on my best friend, and you're still not behind bars where you belong," Kiara defended.

"Oh. Don't mention that lame. He'll never be twice the man that I am. I own the streets of Atlanta, and pretty soon, I shall be the most powerful man that many shall fear. Once we're done with you, then Keith and the rest of your friends will perish, too," Nuke sneered.

"You wanna bet?" a familiar voice chimed in.

Nuke and Todd turned toward the direction of where Keith and the rest of the people were standing. Kiara exhaled, for seeing Keith made her heartbeat like a jackrabbit.

"Oh, looky-looky. If it isn't the lame. Glad you can all join us," Nuke stated in a sly tone.

"Let her go, Nuke! I don't care if we come from the same family tree, but you better not harm Kiara," Keith warned.

"Don't you realize Kiara is your downfall? You could have joined the team. The clubs, women, and money. All of it could have been yours, but you decided to go after this little harlot."

"See, now he had messed up. Beat his behind, Keith! Beat his behind!" Tyshon declared, stomping his feet.

"Oh, that won't be necessary. Take a step closer, and Kiara will be a goner," Nuke threatened, pulling out a nine-millimeter weapon.

"Whoo, Lord, he's gotta a gun," JohnTavis commented before he started to pray in tongues.

"Shut up! Speaking all of that gibberish, your own God can't save you now," Nuke declared.

Smack!

An unfamiliar figure came from behind Nuke and hit him with a bat. She even turned her attention back to Todd, whose eyes appeared as if they would pop out of his sockets.

"You nor your posse will never have control of my life ever

again. Yes, I might be going through a disease, but never under-estimate me. At the end of the day, I am a human being," the woman declared.

"All I got is one thing to say," Tyshon stated.

"What's that?" Malachi wondered, giving Tyshon a confused expression.

"Charge!"

At that moment, everyone raised their bats along with the iron skillet in the air and ran toward their foes. Bats were marking Todd with every beat that connected with his skin. Nuke and Keith engaged in a brawl that involved neither iron skillet. Blow after blow, Keith gathered his strength. Everything around Keith seemed dark, as if it was just him and Nuke on the battlefield.

Kiara watched the intense moment, yet she prayed Keith came out victoriously. Her mind seemed to take a turn as she thought of her son. She couldn't imagine Kyran navigating this cruel world without her. She couldn't imagine missing him driving his first car, going on his first date, and graduating from high school. Kyran was the only child she received from God, and during the moment of life and death, Kyran crossed her mind.

God, if I don't make it out of here alive, please watch over my little boy. I know Keith will take care of him, so please don't allow any harm to come their way, Kiara silently prayed.

Nuke threw Keith back and pointed the nine-millimeter at him. Keith surrendered his hands in the air. Fiery chocolate eyes glared at each other. Blood met the tongue, and the taste of it was unpleasant.

"Only one king can survive in these streets, and that's me.

Tonight, you and your harlot are going to meet your maker," Nuke professed, putting his lanky finger on the trigger.

Bang!

Nuke flinched immediately before falling to the ground. The iron skillet marked him with every blow, for Amelia felt her inner warrior unleashed.

"You lowlife! You had better be glad my father isn't handling you! All it takes is one shot!" Amelia declared, still beating Nuke.

Keith rushed toward Kiara and untied her. He embraced her in a tight hug. Tears streamed down her face as if her eyes were fountains. Pretty soon, the unfamiliar figure stepped in front of them. All eyes were on her as if she was a notorious female pimp. Not a single hair was present on the top of her head.

"I ain't trying to be mean, but who are you?" Stephanie inquired.

"My name is Tiffany, and I am Todd's wife. Well, soon-to-be ex-wife. I am battling cancer, but many can't tell. Yes, I was teaming along with Todd to manipulate many young women like Kiara, but the minute Todd and Nuke started to work together, I backed out. Nuke used to pimp me out on the corner every night for the past ten years. I was putting head to pillow in a different bed every night. I am not innocent, but I can't allow these two to have innocent people fearing for their lives. Kiara, please forgive me," Tiffany explained.

"I already have," Kiara responded.

"Freeze! APD!" Everyone dropped their weapons and surrendered their hands in the air.

"Officer, these young people are innocent. Arrest Nuke and Todd. They kidnapped Kiara," Tiffany explained.

The officer, who came over to Kiara's apartment, appeared with three other police officers, who were sculpted like oxen. They detained Nuke and Todd, but Tiffany was escorted to the car. Everyone soon followed after they secured the bats and iron skillet.

Before driving away from the club, the handsome police officer approached Amelia before she hopped inside of her car. Amelia's chocolate eyes sparkled, and a genuine smile formed across her face.

"Miss, you can now sleep peacefully. The perpetrator has been caught," the officer confirmed.

"Thank you," Amelia said.

"I'm not trying to hold up your time, but I was wondering if you would like to have lunch with me?" the officer requested.

"As much as I would love to, I will be heading back to Hawaii pretty soon. I'm in the Army."

"Will you let me know when you will go back?

"Sure. Have a good night, officer."

The officer smiled at the ebony beauty before walking back to his car. Amelia focused her attention back on Kiara and Keith, as the two continued to embrace one another. Everyone kept their eyes on them and wondered if the two were trying to start a Guinness world record for the longest embrace.

"Keith, I am so sorry for putting you through everything," Kiara apologized.

"Baby, you didn't put me through anything," Keith assured Kiara.

"Keith, I was too foolish and crazy not to realize Todd actually only wanted to make my life a living hell. I thought dating him would only help me get over you, but no matter how hard I tried, I found myself at the crossroad. I wasn't over you even if I tried," Kiara admitted.

Keith reached inside of his pocket and took the ring out of the velvet box. He gently took Kiara's hand and slid the ring on Kiara's finger. Kiara's eyes enlarged as she noticed the luxurious rock on her finger.

"What is this?" She interrogated, turning her attention back to Keith.

"I love you. I love you so much. I can't imagine my life without you or Kyran in it. Will you marry me?"

Kiara gasped, but her feet stood planted to the ground.

"Girl, you better say yes!" Tyshon shouted.

"Girl, you know that boy loves you!" Kydra added.

"He really does!" Sakitta chimed in.

"Keith—" Kiara began.

"Baby, I have been praying God would send you back to me. Grant it, we have so much history and have been through Hell and high water, but none of that means anything if the love is fabricated. Yes, I put God first, but baby girl, you and Kyran are my everything. I don't want to see my son just every other weekend, but I want to come home to my wife and child every day that God allows me to come home to. Please say you'll be my wife."

Kiara glanced into Keith's chocolate eyes. She pictured him walking through the doors of her apartment, and Kyran racing to greet his father. She imagined the lovely evenings of the two of them snuggling cozy on the couch while Kyran snuggled asleep in his bed. She imagined the elegant date nights, but there was a hideous side to marriage. Unexpected nights at the hospital would creep up. Unexpected bills that would escalate like the Empire State building. The fire of pain would lurk them like an intruder, but time would not be on either one's side.

Is it worth it? Will Keith be able to stand by me through good and bad times, in sickness and in health, for richer or poorer, or worse 'til death do us apart? Kiara thought, inhaling and exhaling before giving Keith her final answer.

"Yes, Keith. Yes!" Kiara answered, jumping into his muscular arms.

"They getting married, y'all!" JohnTavis announced.

The rest of the friends cheered and shouted with joy. Keith glanced up toward the sky and mouthed *"Thank you, God,"* for God answered his prayers. Kiara exhaled, yet she didn't think for one second that a chaotic moment would lead her to a happy ending for the night.

Malachi glanced over at Sakitta, who was still performing the Holy Ghost stomp. Feeling she was being spied on, Sakitta noticed Malachi staring back at her. A shy smile appeared on his handsome face, and a sad smile, which appeared on Sakitta's face, greeted Malachi. Malachi migrated toward Sakitta, and Sakitta ceased her stomping and stared at her best friend.

"Hey," Malachi greeted.

"Hey," Sakitta returned.

"Do you want to go somewhere and talk?"

"Sure," Sakitta agreed.

The two migrated from the rest of the group and stopped in front of Malachi's car. Malachi grabbed Sakitta by her hand and gently caressed it. Sakitta kept her focus on Malachi, for everything else around them seemed nonexistent.

"Look, I just want to let you know I am sorry. I mean, grant it, we have history, but sometimes, I do believe we are meant to be friends. I mean, I still think of you when I wake up and even when I go to sleep hoping to dream of you. I mean, like my grandmother always tells me. God does have the last say in the end," Malachi stated.

"Mine tells me that all the time. I mean I will be a fool if I told you that you don't cross my mind when you actually do. I miss being around you, too," Sakitta professed.

"Why don't you call the shots? It's whatever you want to do, and whatever you decide, I'll respect it."

"I love you," Sakitta expressed.

"I love you, too," Malachi returned.

"No, I love *love* you. I don't think I can go a day without you in my life," Sakitta declared.

As soon as Malachi heard the words that escaped from Sakitta's mouth, Malachi's knees buckled, and his heart rate was the speed of a race car. Malachi thought the moment was fabricated by a movie director, but the words that Sakitta voiced weren't written on a script. Leaning toward Sakitta, Malachi allowed his lips to be the lead in a sweet, sensual kiss. Both embraced their arms around each other, for this kiss was the mark of their journey as a couple. As their tongues continued to twirl, all eyes from their friends were eventually on them, and smiles appeared.

Oh, what a night it has been. Amelia thought as she exhaled, knowing that a burden had been lifted off of her shoulder. After the two-minute lip lock, Malachi planted a sweet kiss on Sakitta's forehead.

～

"Mama!" Keith called to his own mother.

Keith's mother appeared through the door, and Kyran poked his head out the door. Kiara ran toward the door and scooped her little boy into her arms. Tears of joy escaped from her, for Kiara couldn't believe she was in the presence of her own child.

"Mommy missed you," Kiara expressed.

"I missed you, too, mommy."

"Kiara, I know I don't see a rock on your finger," Keith's mother pointed out, taking hold of Kiara's left hand.

"Yes, ma'am. I told Keith yes," Kiara relayed.

"See. My baby did what I told him to do. Can I get a whoop whoop?"

"Whoop, whoop!" the gang chorused.

"Keith, we're about to bounce up out of here. We'll call y'all when we get inside," Amelia stated.

"Okay. Mal and Kitta, don't drop those drawers tonight," Keith advised the young couple.

"No, you and Kiara better not drop the drawers until the night of your honeymoon. Okay?" Sakitta blurted out.

Everyone burst into laughter, but pretty soon, everybody migrated to their own perspective places. Keith placed his arm around Kiara's waist, and Kiara placed her head on Keith's shoulder.

I can't believe I am finally going to marry my best friend. This moment seems too surreal, Kiara thought.

"Ladies, I can't believe this day has finally come. My sister and best friend are my maids of honor. Ladies, I decided to do a simple but private wedding. The only people that are not here physically to see this are my father and grandparents," Kiara stated.

Kiara had been waiting for this day to arrive, yet reality kicked in. Like every other young girl who dreamed about their wedding day, Kiara wished her father was there to tell her how beautiful she looked as they migrated to the church, where he would give her away. He would probably give her one last father/daughter father lecture, but God took him away when Kiara was only a teen. Here she was now upgrading from fiancée to wife. Her oldest brother, Kopa, decided to do the honor of giving her away, but it still would not be right. Even worse, it just would not feel right.

"Kiara, I know how much you're missing grandma and grandpa along with dad, but you remember that they are watching over you. They will always be with you in spirit. They want you to enjoy your big day. As a matter of fact, they are in Heaven rejoicing," Amelia reminded Kiara as her arms embraced her in a tight hug.

"Right. If we have to have a moment of silence like those that are no longer here with us, we can do that. You're getting married today, missy," Kenya, Kiara's sister, declared.

All eyes were on Kenya as if this were her time and moment. Although Kiara was close to her sister, Kenya often got under Kiara's skin.

"Kenya, I know I am getting married today, but how would you feel walking in my shoes knowing dad will never walk you down the aisle? How would you feel knowing our grandparents, who supported us especially after mama up and married that sorry lowlife, won't be able to see any of us tie the knot?

Yes, I know I should be happy, but how when the people who really love and care about me are in Heaven?" Kiara defended.

Tears threatened to fall from every woman's face. Every girl dreamed of allowing her father to walk her down the aisle.

"Girl, I hate when that time comes for me to cross that bridge. I never thought I would lose mine at twelve," Kydra stated.

"I am not going to lie, but that was unexpected. Life can be very unexpected," Stephanie chimed in.

All of the girls each grabbed one another's hands and allowed themselves to refresh their minds. The ceremony was about to begin in thirty minutes, but Kiara couldn't help but wish she could bring back the people she adored just for one day. *God, please give me strength.* Kiara silently prayed.

"Y'all, hype me up. I'm nervous as heck," Keith instructed his groomsmen.

"See, as soon as we arrive at the church, I will be up on the stage performing comedy. See, we all need some laughter up in here," Tyshon stated.

"Tyshon, watch what you are going to say up there," Keith reminded.

Keith paced back and forth. His younger brother, Kovi, along with Kiara's older and younger brothers, Kopa and Kion, witnessed Keith being so frantic. JohnTavis hardly said a word but singing could be the best remedy for the moment. Although Kyran assumed this was maybe normal, Kyran observed his father's behavior.

"Dad, are you okay?" Kyran wondered.

"Kyran, listen, son. On the most important day of your life, your nerves will take over. You want everything to be just right, but a mishap will always happen. Pretty soon, your nerves will die down because once you stand hand in hand with the woman that you love. Of course, a wedding is nice to have, but the test comes after the honeymoon — bills, hospital stays, and even late nights will all hinder your marriage, but it is up to you and your wife along with God to stand together amid the storm," Keith lectured.

The words that escaped from Keith's mouth marinated the souls that surrounded him and Kyran. Keith exhaled, yet not a single nerve was attached to him. His signature Colgate smile appeared on his face as he turned and faced the men in the room.

"Fellas, it is showtime," Keith declared. The men, along with Kyran, burst into a roaring of cheers.

CHAPTER 15

"Are you ready?" Kopa inquired, standing side by side with Kiara.

"Yes," Kiara answered, giving her older brother a genuine smile.

Everyone stood at their respective places as they waited for Kiara to make her grand entrance. As soon as "Love Will Find a Way" by Heather Headley played, all eyes were on the elegant bride as she and her brother gracefully strolled down the aisle. The black mermaid dressed hugged Kiara's figure as it outlined her curves with perfection.

Keith tried to keep his composure together, yet tears strolled down his handsome face. He had sunken to his knees, and Kovi placed his hand on Keith's shoulder. Keith wasn't alone, for everyone else allowed tears to fall as well. Keith's mother, along with Amelia's parents, Sakitta and Malachi's grandmothers tried to hold in their composure as well. However, it was indeed this very moment that captured the hearts of the few people in attendance.

"Bro, Kiara is right here," Kovi told Keith.

Keith rose back up. Kiara greeted Keith with a genuine smile and reached out to wipe away his tears.

"Dearly beloved, we are gathered here today to witness the holy matrimony between this young man and woman. Who gives this woman away?" the parson asked.

"I do," Kopa stated proudly.

"Thank you," the parson stated.

Kopa kissed Kiara's cheek and dapped up Keith before standing next to the other groomsmen.

"Very well. If there is any reason these two should not be wedded, let them speak now or forever hold their peace," the parson instructed.

Keith squeezed Kiara's hand, and they both greeted each other with signature smiles. *I can't believe this is finally happening,* Kiara thought.

"Very well—"

"Wait! This wedding is nothing without the bride's mother," a familiar voice spoke.

"You have gotten to be kidding me," Kiara stated in a low tone.

"You should be the last person to show up in here. How you have your own child, and my grandbaby tells me the type of woman you are," Keith's mother fumed.

Nette strolled down the aisle, modeling a midi red dress that outlined her figure. The atmosphere quickly went from sunshine to dark and gloomy. Nette had never had a relation-ship with her children and showing up to Kiara's big day just busted Hell wide open.

"Girl, sit down. This ain't even your wedding. As a matter of fact, aren't my four children happy to see mama?" Nette purred.

"How did you know about the wedding? You were excluded from the list," Kenya questioned. She stepped out of her high heels just in case Nette stepped toward her.

"Look. Don't worry about how I know. You ain't too big to get smack up in here," Nette countered.

"Look! Let me handle this before anyone starts anything," Kiara spoke up.

"Ladies, y'all get ready just in case we gotta pull hair," Keith's mother advised the other ladies.

"Hold up. What part do I play in this?" Major wondered.

"Major, you just sit there and hush," Latoya instructed her husband.

Kiara strolled toward her mother, and her genuine smile disappeared. She stared at the woman, who carried her for nine months, yet her actions told a different story.

"You never really cared about my siblings or me. You thought the world revolves around you, yet you had four mouths that needed to get fed. You became weak because the women that are in the audience are ten times stronger than you. They didn't allow the wood to make them forget about their main responsibility, raising their children," Kiara vented.

"I ain't going to lie, but I ain't had wood in so long," Keith's mother blurted out.

"Mama!" Kovi and Keith interjected.

"Kiara, when your father died, I was lost. I never thought another man will love me. I had needs," her mother defended.

"Somebody is going to have to bail me out because I am about to yank this thang up in here!" Jean declared.

"Grandma, no!" Sakitta rushed toward Jean and grabbed her.

"No! Everyone, listen. Today, there will be a wedding, but I will not be having drama up in here today. Nette, leave. I don't consider you my mother even though you carried me for nine months. My siblings and I had our grandparents, father, and the wonderful people surrounding us today. I forgive you, but you made your bed when choosing your new husband over your four kids. Please leave," Kiara relayed.

"And you better to continue to lie in that bed so that punk can stretch the inside out of you," Major declared.

"Major! Next time, you staying at the house. I ain't taking you anywhere else with me," Latoya proclaimed.

Everyone burst into a chorus of laughter. Amelia couldn't help but glance at her parents, as the wedding could have gone up in flames. Nette's heart shattered into a million pieces, but with no remorse, she strutted out of the church and never once took one last glance at her children.

"I ain't going to lie, but that was better than *Love & Hip Hop,*" the parson blurted out.

"We can carry on with the wedding now," Keith instructed as Kiara rejoined herself with him. Both of their hands entwined with each other, creating a beautiful love sequence with every gentle caress.

"Keith is ready to drop some drawers," JohnTavis teased underneath his breath.

The groomsmen chuckled at the comment, yet Keith glared at them before returning his attention back toward Kiara.

"Very well. Before we go any further, let me remind you

both this. Marriage is very beautiful, yet ugly times will test you. Those ugly times will try to tear you both apart, yet with the Lord in the center of your marriage, you both can overcome those ugly times. Marriage is sacred, for many are unaware that marriage is also a ministry. It is God's design of how man and woman should be. When God created Adam and Eve, he made man first and took one rib from the man in order to create a woman.

Man is the head of the woman, and the woman is the head of children. Christ is the head of man, but God is the head of Christ. Never allow anyone else to come inside your marriage, for it is God, husband, and wife. Husbands are to love their wives as Christ loved the church, and wives are to submit to their husbands," the parson concluded.

"Amen!" Major declared.

"Keith, do you take Kiara to be your lawfully wedded wife to cherish and to hold for better or worse, for richer or poorer, in sickness and in health 'til death do you part?" the parson inquired.

"I will," Keith quickly declared.

The wedding party members giggled.

"Very well. Kiara, do you take Keith to be your lawfully wedded husband, to obey and honor, to cherish and to hold, for better or worse, for richer or poorer, in sickness and in health 'til death do you apart?"

"I will," Kiara answered.

"Now, I know the bride and groom each have their own vows to say to each other, so the floor is all theirs at this very moment."

Kiara gave Kenya the bouquet and turned her attention

toward Keith. She held both of his hands, but she allowed Keith to have the moment first.

"Kiara, I never thought we both would live to see the day to get to this very moment. We started as friends but eventually turned into lovers. Somewhere along the way, we became parents to a little boy, who eventually got both of my ways and looks. Obstacles came along, but slowly God allowed us to find our way back to one another. Love is a gift, but love doesn't exist in fairytales. Love is real, but few know the true meaning of it.

Granted, life is like a seesaw, for there will be more downs than ups. I promise to go to God with you. I promise to be your shoulder to cry on, especially during those rough times. I promise to be honest with you no matter how much the truth hurts. I promise to dance with you in the rain. I promise to forsake all others, for I chose you to be my wife. I promise to have self-control, for disagreements will come along. I promise to be a godly father figure for our son. I promise all of these things to you on this day forward," Keith vowed.

"Keith, you're everything I ever wanted in a man. From play-ground days 'til high school, I never wanted to walk this journey called life without you in it. You are an amazing father to our little boy, and I am blessed for that. The day we broke apart, little did you know you took a piece of my heart with you. I thought our friendship, as well as our love, perished. I thought you would find someone else, who was ten times better than me," Kiara disclosed.

"I couldn't do that, baby. No one could ever take your place. There is no one better than you," Keith declared.

"Whoo!" JohnTavis chorused, imitating a shouting person.

"No matter how hard I tried to get over you, something would not let me. I tried to erase you from my mind, but your image always appeared. Everything came down to you and me, and at the end of the day, I realized I missed my best friend, and no other man will ever do. I promise to honor and cherish you. I promised to go to God with you. I promise to raise our son into a godly man. I promise to be your shoulder to lean on whenever you need. I promise to dance in the rain with you. I promise to be honest with you even when the truth hurts. I promise to forsake all others because I chose you to be my husband. I promise all of these things on this day forward," Kiara vowed.

"With nothing else to say and by the power vested in me, I now pronounce you both husband and wife. You may now kiss the bride," the parson concluded.

Keith cupped both of his hands around Kiara's face, and their lips met in a sensual, sweet kiss. Although the couple tuned out the cheers from their family and friends, there was something significant about this lip-lock. A tingling sensation burned through their bodies, alerting their souls to unite. Their tongues danced together as they were both celebrating the holy matrimony. After the thirty-second kiss, Keith planted a kiss on Kiara's forehead.

"I love you," Keith professed.

"I love you, too," Kiara returned.

Before anyone exited the church, Kyran walked toward his parents, and Keith swooped the little boy up in his arms.

~

"Thank you all for coming out to my wedding. Please drive safely. As a matter of fact, everyone, let me know when you get home. Kyran, please behave while you are with your grandmother. Kitta and Mal, y'all are still too young to be dropping drawers, so wait until the Lord allows you both to become one," Keith relayed to everyone.

"Boy, we know that. Heck. Let's head over to Southside, Kitta," Malachi suggested to Sakitta.

"Grandma, I will make sure that I will be home before midnight," Sakitta told Jean.

"Don't let the switch greet you when you come inside. The only things opened up at midnight are cootie cat and liquor stores," Jean advised Sakitta.

Everyone burst into laughter.

"Are you sure you don't need me to do anything else?" Amelia inquired to Kiara.

"Girl, no. I can't believe I am finally a wife. By the way, give that nice police officer a chance. I'm rooting for you and him," Kiara encouraged.

"Girl, only God has the last say about everything. Besides, I head back to Hawaii in like another week. Long-distance relationships don't always last," Amelia pointed out.

"Well, distance is one thing, but if it's meant to be, then God wanted it to happen. You deserve love. Always remember that."

"I will. Congrats, bestie," Amelia stated, hugging Kiara.

"Thank you."

"Keith, you take care of my best friend. I let y'all know when I get home," Amelia stated, migrating toward her car.

Soon, everyone exited from the church, and Kiara and Keith drove to the Crowne Plaza Hotel. As soon as they both reached the luxurious hotel, Keith went over to the passenger's side and opened the door for Kiara. He extended out his hand, and Kiara accepted it, and Keith gently pulled Kiara out of the car. Closing the door, they both strolled to the desk, yet their hands were still entwined.

"Reservation for Kings," Keith informed the receptionist.

"Alright. Give me one second," the receptionist replied, researching for their names. "Room 113."

The receptionist handed Keith the key, and Keith and Kiara headed to their honeymoon suite.

The moment Keith opened the door, Kiara swiftly grabbed him inside and locked the door. The couple often reminisced about the very first time after high school, but this very moment was unique now that the two were united under God.

The couple shared an intimate kiss as they assisted one another out of their wedding attire and lied back on the bed. Keith planted kisses on Kiara's forehead, eyelids, nose, and lips. He then allowed his soldier to enter inside of her woman cave and stroked her. With each stroke, Kiara allowed a moan to escape. After the deep stroke, Keith pulled out from Kiara and planted a trail of kisses on her stomach.

As soon as his tongue reached her treasure chest, Keith licked then he devoured it. Kiara dug her nails into the sheet as she never knew Keith's tongue game to be on point. As soon as Keith's mouth was full from Kiara's sweet nectar, he embraced his wife.

Love started when two young people, regardless of history, took on a journey that faced many ditches and crossroads. Tonight, love found its way and united two souls into one.

If you enjoyed *Love Will Find a Way Part One,* enjoy a sneak peek of my new standalone, *BabyGirl.*

CHAPTER 1

AISHA

"Girl, I can't believe we are about to graduate!" my best friend, Kijani, exclaimed.

"Girl, we can hear your tail loud and clear! You're louder than me," Samia stated. Samia was my other best friend, too.

"Dang. I really can't believe this is happening. All of us are graduating and pretty soon stepping into the real world," I voiced.

Before I go any further about anything else, let me give you all a proper introduction of myself. My name is Aisha Reynolds, and tonight was the night I climbed the top of the mountain. I, along with my best friends, was graduating from River Dale High. I earned a spot as an honor graduate, for all the different class assignments and late-night projects were worth enduring just to get this moment. I was thankful that my parents and grandparents were here to witness this moment.

The class of 2013 was indeed the smallest class to graduate.

Only one hundred and fifty-five students would receive their diplomas. Listening to the top three graduates giving their speeches only allowed me to take my mind on a different journey. This would be my last summer my friends and I get to make sweet memories before going to separate colleges. Florida Agriculture and Mechanical University would be my new home, especially after visiting the HBCU for my eighteenth birthday weekend. Although my pen game was on point, my primary ambition was to perform on Broadway. I created many great plays but performing them was one major issue. This was one gift I didn't want to waste.

I would definitely miss my friends, for they have always been a shoulder to cry on through the many courses of time. After everything I had been through with my no-good ex, Elijah, I managed to pull through after I called it quits. Elijah chased skirts in the streets like it was his primary assignment, but he failed to realize he was blessed with a keeper.

My writing portfolio impressed the admission counselor at Florida A and M University. My monologue performance of Bernadine from *Waiting To Exhale* raised hairs on the theater staff as well. I didn't know the exact number of times I saw *Waiting to Exhale*, but when I got some time to myself, I watched it and placed my shoes in the feet of the four heroines. Florida wasn't new to me, for my family and I traveled there for family reunions. I was ready to embark on a new journey, yet my friends and I weren't ready to cross that bridge yet.

"Can these folks hurry? All of us have a party to attend at a house on a hill," Tongai stated.

"Patience is a virtue, young man," I quoted, for my voice was soft as a feather.

After hearing the long speeches and receiving our diplomas, it was time to get our groove on. I wanted to have the most memorable summer with my friends, for we might not get another chance. We were all headed to different cities and colleges, and tonight marked the end of our high school careers.

I migrated to hug a few of my classmates, but I froze dead in my tracks. A muscular stranger, whose smooth dark chocolate skin, which made my mouth water stood ten feet from me. His muscular chest sculpted perfectly through his shirt. His haircut was a top fade, and his pearly whites took my breath away.

God, where have I seen this man from? I wondered, turning away. I knew my grandparents and parents were waiting for me to come. I noticed a few of my friends taking pictures with their families. Before I could take another step, a strong grip on my arm caught my attention.

"Where are you going?" a familiar voice snarled at me.

God today is supposed to be the best day of my life. Why is this lowlife here? I thought, reluctantly turning around and seeing the last person I wanted to see.

"Make it fast, Elijah," I demanded, fighting out of his grip.

"Congratulations to you, baby," Elijah stated rudely.

"Let me go! There is nothing there anymore. You made your choice when you decided to go and mess with Tasha. I am not the one that will fight another female over a no-good worthless man. Heck, if I wanted revenge, I wouldn't have walked across the stage today. Heck. Bossing up on you is my way of getting revenge. You ain't got nothing going for yourself, and the last thing I need from you is to bring me down where you are at.

You better let me go before I get the police on you for harassing me."

Elijah's eyes grew wide as saucers. The words that spewed out of my mouth shot like arrows through his chest. He gripped my arm tighter, yet I wasn't going to backdown. Before I could get out of his grip by using Plan B, the same guy I saw from afar rushed over to my aid.

"Aye, punk! Let her go!" he warned.

"And, if I don't…" Elijah challenged.

Wham!

Within a blink of an eye, the guy's fist met Elijah's left jaw. Elijah tumbled to the ground, losing his balance. The guy was ready to pounce on Elijah, but Kojo immediately went toward him to stop him from doing any more damage.

"Enoji, don't do it, man. He is not worth it. You just got home, dude," Kojo advised.

"Enoji?" My chocolate eyes sparkled as soon as I turned my attention to him.

"It's I, baby girl. By the way, congratulations," Enoji stated, giving me a forehead kiss.

My heart raced like a jackrabbit. Enoji was only four years older than me, but there wasn't a single moment I thought about Enoji. We had a unique friendship, yet some would label it platonic. Now that I was eighteen, I could date anyone I wanted, minus men that are taken, but my high standards were going to intimidate some men who came my way.

"When did you get here?"

"Earlier today. What are you doing tonight?"

"The crew will be coming over to my place. As a matter of

fact, why don't you come over to my place? It has been forever since I have seen you," I invited.

"Sure. I was going to swing by there anyway," Enoji assured me.

In the moment, as we stood there, a fiery chemistry burned in the midst. Our chocolate eyes stared deeply at one another, yet it seemed as if we were glancing through the windows of our souls. I did my best not to blush, but Enoji's sexy smile turned me on.

"Aisha, we are ready to leave," my mother called from behind.

"I'll see you in a bit," I told Enoji.

"Alright, baby girl," Enoji stated, causing me to blush a little more.

I did my best to walk straight. I had to pull a front and not leave any trace of talking to Enoji.

We escaped the mass crowd and migrated toward the 2013 Camry. As soon as I hopped inside, I couldn't help but to think of Enoji. The day he left to go to Morehouse College shattered my soul like Hell. After I discovered Elijah's infidelity, I wished Enoji was there to be my shoulders to lean on. I am preserving myself for marriage, but I wanted to be near Enoji. I wanted to feel secure in his strong, muscular arms. I wanted him to whisper powerful affirmations in my ear. Most importantly, I wanted his lips to plant lingering kisses on my forehead. I cherished a forehead kiss more than a deceitful sensual lip-lock.

"Aisha, why was that guy on the ground?" my mother, Lavanya, inquired.

"Enoji knocked out Elijah because Elijah would not let go of my arm. By the way, who invited Elijah? I surely didn't. I mean, why did Elijah have to come on the night of my graduation? This is supposed to be the best night of my life," I stated.

"Hon, whenever you boss up, just remember this. New devils, new levels. There will always be that one person who will always try to sabotage you because God put you in a position that might be a few elevations from where he or she might be. Not everyone you meet is a friend or enemy, but at the end of the day, you must watch your surroundings at all times," my mother advised.

My parents feared the Lord, so it was essential I got the same teaching. No matter what grade I was in, I read the Bible before class started. My friends noticed it and always respected my moment with the Lord. Eventually, my friends began to get their relationship with Christ on point, especially since college will be loaded with a lot of temptation. I wondered what college life would be like since I was migrating to another state. I promised my friends I would keep in touch with them.

The ride to our two-story estate seemed shorter than usual. I only lived almost thirty minutes away from the high school. As soon as my father parked the car, we hopped out and raced toward the house. I rushed upstairs to my room. Placing my cap and gown on my bed, I glanced in the mirror and admired my beautiful figure. The strapless glittery dress didn't reveal too much, but it outlined my curves. My dark chocolate skin had an angelic glow. My natural hair cooperated with the heat, yet they never got along with one another.

"Aisha," my father, Mojo, alerted me.

"Father, you scared me. How long have you been standing there?" I wondered, yet my heart raced like a jackrabbit.

"A little over a minute. So tell me. How does it feel to be a high school graduate?" my father inquired.

I could look through those deep chocolate eyes of my father and feel that he was going to miss me. I often clung to him for advice, but now that I was going to be eight hours away from home, I felt the pain that pierced my father's heart. I was no longer the little girl who would go to him for anything. I was looking forward to college and seeing what else was out there. My father was overprotective of his family, and many people feared him — well, often. Once people got to know him, their internal judgment of my father would vanish.

"Surreal. Father, I never thought this day would come. I mean, the crew and I are looking forward to spending the summer together one more time. To tell you the truth, I am going to miss school," I admitted.

"More like you are going to miss your friends. Aisha, you will meet new people when you go to college. You and your friends can still keep in touch with each other. The real world is a whole new world, and reality will definitely be the harsh truth. Friends come and go," my father told me.

"Father, I get that, but that statement should be for men coming in and out of my life. I just ran into an ex-boyfriend of nightmares past. I mean, my friends were there for me once I discovered his acts of infidelity. I sometimes wished I'd never given any of my time to that lowlife."

"Answer me this question. What did you see in that fool?"

"I wanted to see Elijah for his worth. I have always been infatuated with guys that have street swag, but I feel as if there is always a soft spot in them. Not everyone appears to be big and bad," I reminded my father.

"My days of being that young knucklehead might be over with, but the streets never left me internally. I don't know about Enoji. I mean, the boy seems okay. If he ever hurts you, December will have a joyous time with him."

A smile did not form on my face, yet the words that spat out of my father's mouth made my blood boil. Enoji might not have been perfect, but the streets did not fascinate him. At the end of the day, I wanted to enjoy a moment with my family and friends. I didn't want to have a moment where I felt my father was passing judgment on Enoji. Whenever I was around Enoji, I felt as if we were the only two people in the world. His beautiful affirmations gave me butterflies, and my beautiful Colgate smile would appear.

"Dad, can we have this conversation at another time? I mean, this should be about me, not you bringing up Enoji and stereotyping him as if he is a criminal. Why don't you do that to Elijah instead?"

My father's face presented a scowl, and he brushed away whatever he was going to say. I knew my father only wanted what was best for me, but I always thought with the head on my shoulder instead of the power portal between my legs.

"Aisha, your friends are here!" my mother called.

"Coming, mother," I replied.

"Remember, this conversation is not over. I just want you to make the right choice. You are the only daughter we have, and please don't do anything I wouldn't do."

I migrated out of my bedroom and headed downstairs to join my friends. I strolled gracefully like a princess down the staircase, for all eyes were on me. This really wasn't my night, but my friends also endured this journey, so we're going to celebrate as well. Summertime was right around the corner, and our goal was to create memories where we could reminisce once we reach middle age.

"Girl, it is about time you come downstairs. What was taking you so long?" Samia wondered.

"Girl, my father was giving me the talk. You know he is going to miss me."

"Girl, you ain't lying about that. Shoot, if I had a father like yours, girl, I wouldn't know what to do. Mine is always on the road," Samia stated.

More Coming Soon...